JUDGE RANDALL GETS IT WRONG

JUDGE RANDALL
GETS IT WRONG

TONY ROGERS

A Judge Randall Mystery

Other titles in the Judge Randall series:

ISBN: 978-1-7356835-6-0 (Paperback)
ISBN: 978-1-7356835-7-7 (Ebook)

Published by Quinn Cove Books

Cover Design by Berge Design

to Tamara

1

In Judge Randall's sixty-nine years, he had met very few self-critical men – plenty of smug men with insatiable egos, plenty of oblivious men who wouldn't recognize themselves if they bumped into themselves on the sidewalk, plenty of talented men who handled the world with skill and aplomb but had no idea what was going on inside their psyches. Now and then Jim would meet a young man who seemed to know he had an inner life even if he didn't yet know quite what it was, a young man such as Aaron Winters.

Winters was a senior at MIT, majoring in math and computer sciences. They met for the first time at The Long Gone, a coffee shop halfway between MIT and Harvard that had become Jim's de facto chambers since he retired from the Massachusetts Superior Court four years ago.

Aaron Winters didn't seem happy to be there. He had short dark hair, the kind you run your fingers through once in the morning and don't need to touch again all day. He was slight in build, and his smile came with training wheels. He sat across from Jim.

The interior of The Long Gone received little natural light, and the sunlight that made it through the front windows quickly met its match from the glow of a dozen laptops. "I'm only here because my father insisted I meet you," Aaron said.

"Relax, I know why you're here. Your father is worried about you. He says you are about to throw your education away and thinks I may be able to talk you out of it. Your father and I go way back. We knew each other in college."

"He told me. He said he would never have guessed that you would become a judge."

"Whereas I felt sure your father would become an eminent mathematician. He seemed to exist in a different realm than the rest of us. Let me ask you a question: did you choose math as a major to please your dad?"

"To please him? No, to get him off my back. I enjoy math, but I don't want to make a career out of it."

"Understood. What are you thinking of doing?"

"Urban planning or politics, both of which drive Dad bonkers."

"Why?"

"Because they are messy and imprecise and human. He likes clear-cut answers, the kind only numbers...."

Aaron stopped in mid-sentence. An expression came over his face that scared the hell out of Jim.

"What's wrong?" Jim asked, looking where Aaron was looking.

A beer-bellied man with a deeply rutted face and a gun was approaching their table. His face was a dirt road over which heavy trucks had repeatedly driven. He stopped in front of Aaron.

"Come with me." The gunman waved his gun.

"Oh, no," Aaron exclaimed, sotto voce.

Jim stayed seated. "Want to tell me what's going on?"

The usual low murmur in The Long Gone had ceased. Two or three people continued talking until they too noticed what was happening. Then total silence, not even the hiss of steam from the espresso machine.

Aaron got to his feet. "Tell Dad..."

The gunman didn't let Aaron finish. "Shut up! Move!" The gunman didn't seem into his job. He growled the right words and waved his gun menacingly, but seemed to be following a script.

A moment later the gunman and Aaron Winters were gone, as if they had never been there. No one in The Long Gone moved or spoke. Then, suddenly, chaos. "Call the cops! Somebody call the cops!"

*

Jim Randall sat in the office of Assistant DA Ted Conover, his longtime friend and former courtroom nemesis. Ted had looked like a newborn when he first argued a case in Jim's courtroom. He had aged in the twenty years since, but still looked youthful – gravitas worn lightly. Ted's office hadn't changed a whit: same family pictures on the desk, same faded painting of a sailboat on the wall behind his desk. Ted had won many awards during his legal career, but you couldn't tell from his plain and simple office. Jim sometimes wondered what would happen if he moved a picture while Ted was out of the room: a minor freak out? A total meltdown? (In keeping with Ted's low-key manner, both would be hard to notice.)

"What struck me the most was that the gunman made no attempt to hide his face – no mask, no hoodie, a man in his fifties with beer belly and gun, strolling into a coffee shop and abducting a young man, as if it happened every day."

"And then what?" Ted asked from behind his desk.

"Aaron and the gunman walked out together, but not before Aaron started to say, 'tell Dad....'"

"What did you make of that?" Ted asked.

"Was he asking me to tell his father he had been kidnapped? Could be, but something about Aaron's tone – resigned, weary, pugnacious – made me think it was more than that. It was payback of a sort."

"Payback? How could that be?"

"I don't know. It makes no sense, but that's how it sounded to me."

"Did you previously know young Winters?"

"No. I've known his father, Edgar Winters, since college; Edgar was concerned about Aaron's future and asked me to talk to him."

"Have you spoken to the father since the incident?"

"Yes, I called him immediately, and I'm heading to his office after I leave here. He's a prominent professor at MIT. Rumor has it that he's next in line for a Nobel Prize."

"What was his reaction to the kidnapping?"

"Muted concern. Hoped Aaron was okay, said all the right things, but I got the impression he was more concerned with how the kidnapping might affect his reputation."

"Full of himself, I take it."

"Overflowing."

Jim liked to walk. He walked everywhere he could. The walk from Ted Conover's office to MIT was so brief it didn't count as a walk. MIT doesn't name its buildings, it numbers them. Edgar Winters's office was in E73, on the edge of campus across a city street from the MIT power plant.

Edgar Winters in person gave the impression of a man who couldn't tear himself away from the fascinating things that were going on inside his mind in order to pay attention to the person he was talking to. His expression barely changed as Jim recounted the kidnapping of his son.

"And that's all I know. I wish I could tell you more. Your son and I were just starting to talk when the gunman entered and forced Aaron to leave with him. This must be agonizing for you."

"Of course, he's my son, but we weren't close. We rarely spoke."

"You and Aaron rarely spoke?"

"Yes. We've never been close, but lately he has drifted even farther away from me. That's why I asked for your help. I thought you had a better chance of persuading him to do the right thing than I did."

"You implied he was about to throw his future away. What specifically did you mean?"

"Aaron has always been a top student, but lately he has let his grades slip. I warned him that letting his grades slide his senior year sent a clear signal to grad schools that he didn't care."

"How did he respond?"

"He said he was rethinking his future. Said he was sorry if he disappointed me."

"The Long Gone's surveillance camera captured a clear image of the kidnapper. His picture has been widely circulated. It won't be long before he's captured. Do you have any idea why this happened?"

Winters bristled. "Absolutely not! How could I? What are you implying?"

"I'm not implying anything. Had your son said or done anything recently that would give us a clue? Something that escaped your notice at the time but in hindsight sheds light?"

"I have always thought that he blamed me in some way for his mother's death. Maybe that attitude has been more pronounced recently."

"How old was he when his mother died?"

"Thirteen. She died of an infection that reached her heart. Twenty-four hours and she was gone. Aaron never got over it." Winters paused. "I did my best to be a good father, but I couldn't possibly be his mother too."

"Who can I talk to who knows about his recent life?"

"His ex-fiancée, Melanie Johnson. She and Aaron had planned to get married after Aaron graduated, but they called it off not long ago."

"Any idea why?"

"None."

"Where can I find her?"

"She graduated from MIT last semester. I occasionally saw them walking together on campus before she graduated, but I only talked to her once or twice. She's not up to his standards. Aaron could do better. I believe she's working in Burlington, Vermont."

When Jim left Professor Winters's office, he roamed the MIT campus imagining Aaron attending classes on this industrial-strength campus where his father was a living legend. The MIT buildings embody purpose: here we build and discover they seem to say; we don't endlessly debate esoterica. An unforgiving campus. How could the younger Winters compete with his old man on a campus tailor-made for Professor Winters?

When Jim tired of imagining himself into the life of Aaron Winters, he walked the two miles home. As he neared Harvard Square, he called Pat – Patricia Knowles, former colleague on the Massachusetts Superior Court bench and since they retired, his significant other and de facto partner in crime fighting. They spent most nights together but kept separate residences. Her apartment was on Beacon Hill, Jim's townhouse was in Cambridge. "Hi, I'm heading home. Your place or mine tonight?"

2

A text from Ted arrived while Jim and Pat were eating breakfast in Jim's sun-filled kitchen next morning.

We have identified Aaron
Winters's abductor. Call me.

"So who's the villain?" Jim asked when he reached Ted.

"Good morning, Jim. The villain is a small-time crook named Micky Owens, a fuck-up who does dirty work for the big boys. Fifty-seven years old, recently granted compassionate release from Concord State Prison because he has only a few months to live. Had been serving four years for aggravated assault, the latest in a long string of petty and not so petty crimes."

"Has there been a ransom demand?"

"No. Not yet."

"Why would a petty thief kidnap a promising student like Aaron Winters, if not for ransom?"

"For a paycheck. Somebody paid him to do it."

"What sticks in my mind is that Owens made no attempt to cover his face, as if he didn't care if he was caught."

When Jim got off the phone, his expression mixed grit and huh? Pat knew the look well. "You're going to follow up on this, aren't you?"

"Now why would you think that?"

*

Boston to Burlington, Vermont, by car takes three and a half hours, I-93 to I-89, interstate all the way. Jim and Pat split the driving. They were on their way to interview Melanie Johnson, the ex-fiancée of Aaron Winters.

"I can drive again if you get tired," Jim said.

"I'm doing fine," Pat replied. "Relax."

"I keep seeing Micky Owens walking into The Long Gone with a gun like it was an everyday occurrence. Given how wasted he looked, I'm amazed he had the strength to hold a gun." They were passing the turnoff for Montpelier, the Vermont state capital. "Montpelier is where Joyce and I got married."

"Your Joyce and my Ed died within a few months of each other," Pat didn't take her eyes off the road as she drove. A tractor-trailer blew by on her left, kicking up mist as it went.

Jim replied, "Joyce and I took it slow, I remember, which in retrospect was the right thing to do."

When Jim and Pat reached Burlington, their hotel room overlooked Lake Champlain and the distant Adirondack Mountains. Jim was at home with water views – the view from his Vermont house was of the Connecticut River and its sheltering valley.

"The coffee shop where we're meeting Melanie Johnson is a short walk uphill from the hotel," Jim said as they unpacked their overnight bags.

Melanie Johnson turned out to be barely five feet tall. Jim and Pat – both close to six feet – towered over her. Melanie wore jeans and a loose-fitting T shirt.

"Don't get up," Jim said as he and Pat approached her table. The spiffy coffee shop was nothing like The Long Gone. "This is Pat Knowles, I'm Jim Randall."

"I'm Melanie Johnson." They shook hands.

"Thanks for meeting with us," Jim said.

"You said something in your email about being with Aaron when he was kidnapped. Is that true?" Melanie had the diffident face of someone who didn't pass judgment on people right away but judged firmly when the time came.

"Yes, it is. Aaron and I had just started talking when a man with a gun told Aaron to come with him. I'm hoping that knowing more about Aaron will help me understand why it happened. That's where you come in. Aaron's father told me you and Aaron were engaged to be married."

Melanie averted her eyes whenever she began talking. As she gained confidence, she shifted gears and stared directly at whomever she was talking to. Jim found the habit mildly unnerving. "We were. We called off the engagement shortly before Aaron was kidnapped."

"Did the kidnapping have anything to do with ending the engagement?"

Immediately, sharply. "No! Are you out of your mind? How could it?"

"Never mind. Ignore that." Jim had been fishing and didn't expect her to say yes, but was a little surprised by her vehemence.

Pat tried to smooth the waters. "It must be especially hard to take happening so soon after you two called off your engagement. You must feel guilty, even though you obviously had nothing to do with the kidnapping."

Melanie nodded. "Yes, you understand. I've looked for a connection, but we hadn't told anyone about our breakup except Aaron's dad. I hadn't even told my mom."

"Could Aaron have told others without you knowing?"

"I guess anything is possible, but it wouldn't be like Aaron to tell others. He kept everything inside."

Jim spoke. "Was Aaron in some kind of trouble?"

"You don't understand MIT students. There are always problem sets to do. One of the things I remember from my student days there were the endless discussions about problem sets, even at meals. I made it through school by becoming a nervous wreck, Aaron made getting good grades look easy. No, he wasn't in some kind of trouble. He didn't have time to get into trouble."

"Is there anything Aaron said or did, anything you are aware of, that could provide a hint as to why someone would kidnap him?" Jim asked.

"No, that's what baffles me most. To have him disappear is bad enough, but not knowing why makes it so much worse."

Pat asked, "It sounds to me as if you two were devoted to each other. Is there a chance you'll get back together if he is found?"

That coaxed a sad smile from Melanie. "I very much hope so."

Jim had one more question. "How well do you know Aaron's father?"

"Not well, but to the extent I did, I couldn't stand him. Professor Winters is kind to numbers but contemptuous of people. All Aaron wanted was to be understood by his father, all Professor Winters wanted was for Aaron to make him look good. Reflected glory, any kind of glory."

Pat said, "But Aaron was about to graduate with honors from the school where his father teaches. One would think that would satisfy the professor."

Melanie replied, "One would think. But Aaron knew that having second thoughts about math as his career would horrify his father. Aaron sees numbers as problem-solving tools, his father sees numbers as the elixir of life. Aaron complained to me that if he could be written as an equation, his father would like him much better."

"You've been very helpful," Jim said. "We're staying at the Lakeside Inn tonight. If you think of anything else, give us a call."

"I will, but I've told the FBI everything I know. Wait, there's one thing you can tell me that the police can't. How did Aaron react when the gunman pulled a gun on him? Was he terrified? I hate to think of Aaron terrified."

"Angry, startled, but not terrified. His reaction surprised me. The sudden appearance of a gun scared me and others in the coffee shop more than it scared Aaron."

She nodded. "I'm relieved. Whatever he's done, he doesn't deserve to suffer. He's a good person. Too sensitive for his own good sometimes, but kind of heart."

The coffee house was on the cusp of a pedestrian street high above the lake. Jim and Pat walked downhill to their hotel when they left Melanie Johnson. The sun was bright off the water.

"What do you think?" he asked Pat.

"She still loves Aaron. She'd take him back in a second."

"Really? I sensed a cooling on her part."

"Lucky for the world that your duties as a judge didn't include couples counseling."

"Madam, I scoff. My romantic advice can't be beat."

Pat replied, "You scoff, I chortle."

"We should hang out a shingle: Chortle and Scoff – Attorneys at Law."

She took his hand. "The lake's pretty, isn't it?"

"Yes, it is."

"You've put ideas into my head."

"Of what to name our law firm?"

"Of what we could do before dinner."

Jim held her gaze for a moment. "Madam, no one would believe that the stern person on the bench could be so ribald."

She dropped his hand. "I was not stern, I was beloved. And I have never been called ribald in my life, I hate that word. Horny? Yes, very, but ribald? Never."

"Yes, ma'am."

They reached the hotel. Pat hadn't spoken for a half-block. As they passed the front desk on the way to the elevator, Jim asked her, "Still interested?"

"In what?"

"You know."

"I want you to say it."

"You're embarrassing me."

She tugged his arm. "Say it or forget it."

"Still interested in sex?"

"In the abstract or with you?"

"Oh, hell! Do you want to jump in the sack and throw statute and case law to the winds?"

"That's better. Makes me feel ribald."

Jim swiped the doorlock with the key card. "Get ready to lose your honor, Your Honor."

They ate dinner at a French bistro at the tail end of the pedestrian street. The wine was serviceable and cheap. The food neither excited nor disappointed.

Sipping a Ventoux, Jim reviewed the day. "Morning, inconclusive. Afternoon, va va voom. Evening so so, so far. Do you think Melanie Johnson knows more about the kidnapping than she's letting on?"

"Yes. You?"

"Me too. I accept your assessment that she'd take him back in a second, but her reaction to the kidnapping struck me at times as rehearsed."

They undressed and got into bed. Pat immediately opened the book she had been reading. Jim lay on his back with his hands beneath his head. "Want to know my theories of the case?" he asked a few minutes later.

Pat lowered her book but said nothing. Jim took that as a yes.

"Theory #1: Someone as yet unknown kidnapped Aaron for ransom. No ransom demand has yet been made, but that's not unusual. Ransom demands are often made after enough time has passed to scare the hell out of relatives. Theory #2: Professor Winters orchestrated the kidnapping to teach his son a lesson: see what happens when you challenge me, son? Theory #3: Aaron orchestrated his own kidnapping to scare his father into leaving him alone. Trouble with that theory, I don't think that Professor Winters cares enough about his son to be scared by his abduction, which Aaron would have known. Which also suggests why theory #1 won't work – if there's a ransom demand, Professor Winters will probably try to bargain the amount down as close as possible to zero, and if the amount's still too much, tell the kidnappers to keep the kid."

Pat patted Jim on the head. "Go to sleep, Jim. You will think more clearly in the morning."

"Are you implying I'm not thinking clearly now?"

"I'm implying I want to finish my book. Goodnight, sweet sleuth."

3

Enrique Montgomery was the high-energy, low-key head of the FBI's Boston bureau. He dressed casually, often wearing jeans with his blue blazer. He had only been in his job for a few years. Jim called Enrique from the car while Pat drove home the next day.

"Hello, Jim. Where have you been?" Enrique said.

"Solving cases."

"Without me? Improbable. How can I help you?"

"I'm calling about the Aaron Winters kidnapping. Are you familiar with that?"

"Yes, Ted Conover asked us to lend a hand. Given the tight geography of New England, it's very possible that Winters was transported across a state line after the kidnapping. I've read the account you gave the Cambridge police. Do you have something new?"

"Pat and I are on our way home from Burlington, Vermont, where we talked to Winters's ex-fiancée. What I was trying to determine is whether she was involved in the kidnapping."

"And what did you conclude?"

"She and Winters had called off their engagement before the kidnapping. My opinion – my guess – is that she knows more than she's telling us. Maybe she's talked to Aaron since the kidnapping and knows where he is, for example. But I have no evidence to back that up."

"Your opinions matter, Jim. You assessed the credibility of countless witnesses who appeared before you in court. Very few have your experience."

"True, but I'm not always right."

"Humility? From the great Judge Randall?"

"I reserve a few minutes each week for humility. Good for the soul. Any leads on the whereabouts of Micky Owens?"

"None so far. He has done a pretty effective disappearing job."

"With his victim. Both are missing. Please keep me informed if you find anything new."

Jim rode in silence for miles. The interstate hypnotically rose and fell over the hills of Vermont. Jim fought sleep.

"Jim," he heard someone say in the distance.

It was Pat, in the driver's seat. "Don't fall fast asleep. I may want you to drive at some point."

Jim sat up straight. "I'm awake. I'll drive whenever you want."

They arrived at Jim's townhouse without switching drivers. "You seemed tired," Pat explained when Jim asked why.

"I wasn't tired, I was wondering whether Aaron Winters is still alive. The longer this goes without a ransom demand being made, the more I wonder."

Pat squeezed the car into Jim's skinny garage. Pat climbed out while Jim retrieved their overnight bags from the trunk. "Micky Owens had recently been released from Concord Prison." Jim dumped the bags in the kitchen. "I think I'll pay the prison a visit, and see what I can learn."

MCI-Concord sits on a traffic circle just past the center of Concord, once upon a time the home of Henry David Thoreau. Jim found it hard to believe that Walden Pond and the red-brick and barbed wire prison were in the same town. The prison's watch towers have a good view of the ceaseless traffic bunching up at the rotary (or circle, if one is from out-of-state). Jim liked the rotary because it marked the end of the heaviest traffic when he drove to his Vermont house. Past the rotary the road sped up, in a manner of speaking, though the traffic bunched up again near the small towns that hugged the road.

Jim announced himself at the guard's office. Jim had never found prisons as depressing as expected, mainly because he knew he could leave when he wanted. Still, the amount of security was daunting.

The warden was expecting him. "Skip Lockhardt was Micky Owens's cellmate. He is willing to meet with you," the warden said as he led Jim down the hall to a visitors' room.

"What's Lockhardt in for?" Jim asked as they walked.

"Originally spousal abuse, then murder of a guard. Bad dude. He has nothing to lose by talking to you. He's not getting out of here."

Jim was led into a small room with a table in the middle. Lockhardt was sitting at the table. A guard kept watch by the door.

Lockhardt looked to be in his sixties. Prison had leached the color from his face long ago, yet there was enough anger in his eyes to suggest he was still alive. "How are you?" Jim asked.

"About the same as yesterday and the day before and the day before, and so on and so on. Not bad. And you?"

"As I'm sure the warden told you, I'm interested in learning more about Micky Owens. You and he were cellmates, is that right?"

"Yes, when I was released from solitary, he and I shared a cell for several months. Between you and me, he was nuts."

"How so?"

"He adored hard men, aspired to be one himself, wanted to know all my tricks. I told him some that were true, and some I made up. Making stuff up helps to pass the time around here, God knows we've got plenty of it."

"I assume you heard what he did recently."

Lockhardt shook his head in disbelief. "Kidnapped a college kid out of a crowded coffee shop. Stupid shit. Sounds like Micky."

"Knowing Micky, do you think it was his idea?"

Lockhardt made a sound that was a cross between a snort and a laugh. "Micky? Not a chance. He was put up to this, not a shadow of a doubt in my mind."

"Any idea why someone would put him up to something so dumb?"

"Revenge. Ransom. For the hell of it. Take your pick."

"Any idea who?"

"Not a clue. Why would I know that?"

"You strike me as the kind of guy who makes it his business to know everything."

"You flatter me. I'm just a lowly con, living out my days." He smiled, pleased with his turn of phrase. "You wouldn't guess it, but an MIT student is teaching me coding. He comes in once a month for an hour. Best hour of my sad existence. If I ever get out of here, I'll know a trade. Course, I'm never getting out of here." He sighed and smiled.

"There's always the possibility of pardon if you're a model prisoner."

"That rules me out." Lockhardt's smile faded. "Do you know the last time I saw the outside world?"

"You tell me."

"Twenty-five years ago. My wife's funeral. Our kids were there, haven't seen them since."

"How long were you married?"

"Bobbie and I met in high school. I dropped out in junior year. She was in love with me, so we eloped. We had our first kid while she was still in school. That's the one thing I'd do over if I could. Be a good husband to her, she deserved better than me."

Lockhardt fell silent. The transformation in his eyes from the beginning of the interview was startling. From defiant to defeated, from wise guy to widower.

Jim left the prison profoundly shaken, by the waste of life a prison represents, by the sheer insanity of a wife abuser wishing he had been a better husband, as if his failing was forgetting to buy his wife a birthday present.

How did I endure coming face-to-face with this side of humanity on a daily basis when I was a judge, Jim asked himself as he walked to his car. It was my job then, that's how. He had been able to compartmentalize. He was out of practice. The law abiding and law breakers blended together in his mind now.

He had forgotten where he parked his car. He stopped walking and searched the lot. All the cars looked the same. If a simple thing like forgetting where your car is parked can cause mild panic, what would being locked up cause?

Where had he parked the car? Idiot, it had been close by all the time. He crossed over one row of cars to where he had parked, climbed in and sat still until his breathing settled, then drove out of the lot to freedom.

*

Jim stayed at Pat's that night. They didn't have a strict routine of where to stay, but for the most part they alternated nights. They ate dinner at Pat's.

Pat's kitchen windows looked out on a narrow city garden crowded with bushes which shielded the garden from neighbors. The dominant theme of the view was the red of the brick townhouses; the secondary theme, the green of shrubbery.

"I am finding this investigation especially vexing, which I don't understand." Jim was still on his first glass of wine. He kept an ample supply of his favorite wines from the Languedoc at Pat's apartment.

"Any guess why?"

"Because I have so little to go on. I saw an abduction happen, but I know less about it than about any other case I've investigated. Which suggests that it's a bad thing to investigate a crime you witnessed."

"Somehow I knew you had a theory." Pat looked amused.

"Don't smirk. You always smirk when I think out loud," Jim said.

"What you think is a smirk is a look of affection." She lifted her wine glass in his direction. "To my ardent lover, who hides his feelings so well I never have any idea of what he's feeling."

"See? You did it again. A smirk. Stop it."

Pat clicked glasses. "Cheers."

He slept soundly that night, happy to be with Pat. She provided his center of gravity. When he was with her, he could locate his true north, and with that, other parts of his life fell into place. Like what lead to follow next. In the morning, he texted Aaron's father, Edgar, and asked to see him again.

In his reply, Professor Winters said to drop by his office late morning, although he seemed baffled by the request.

In certain slants of light, the MIT campus looked spectral, haunted. Like the ruins of an ancient civilization on another planet.

As Jim entered Professor Winters office, Winters seemed not to remember who Jim was. Jim reminded him.

"Jim Randall, I'm here about your son."

"Yes, of course." Winters gestured to a chair. "Have you heard from him?"

"No, I was wondering if you had."

"Not a word. He has done this before."

"Been kidnapped?"

"No, disappeared for days or weeks when the going got tough. I think this time he's afraid what will happen after graduation. Real world, you know. Aaron lacks tensile strength."

Jim tried another tack. "Professor, your son was abducted at gunpoint. He didn't vanish voluntarily."

Winters made a face. "I suppose, but Aaron is not brave. He won't live up to his promise if he continues ducking when the going gets tough."

"You're not worried about his safety?"

"Worried? No. Why should I be?"

Jim was aghast. "Because he was abducted at gunpoint!"

"Aaron's always had a flare for the dramatic. It's how he avoids blame. It's his refuge, his escape hatch."

"The gun looked like the real deal to me, Professor, as did the man carrying it."

Winters shrugged. "I'll worry when I think worry is warranted."

Unbelievable, Jim mused when he left Winters's office. Winters had originally asked Jim to talk to Aaron about his future, but seemed unconcerned now that Aaron had been kidnapped, lending credence to Jim's theory #2, that Professor Winters knew his son was safe because he, Professor Winters, had staged the kidnapping. But the simpler explanation was that Professor Winters was a terrible human being, more concerned with how well Aaron's life reflected on him than whether Aaron was well. Perhaps prospective fathers should have to pass an aptitude test. Jim and his late wife, Joyce, had wanted kids, but in retrospect, Jim thought things had worked out for the best.

He lived too much inside himself to be a good father. Was too fond of his own thoughts. But he would have been a better father than Edgar Winters.

Maybe Winters was losing his mind, maybe that was the explanation for his shocking lack of concern. Or maybe he *had* staged the whole thing. As a general rule, Jim preferred to start with simple explanations and add complexity as needed. Winters was an unfit father, that much was self-evident. Jim would stick with that for the time being.

Jim didn't have the energy to walk home so he waited for the #1 bus. It came in four minutes. As usual, the bus contained as eclectic a mix of people as one could imagine. The variety of skin tones could be used as paint chips in a hardware store, the ages of riders ranged from stroller to walker, the expressions on faces ranged from scholarly to raving. One scary man blocked half the rear exit and taunted riders as they disembarked.

The scary man looked vaguely familiar. Jim couldn't get a good look without being obvious, but the glimpses he got reminded Jim of Micky Owens. Micky Owens of the deeply rutted face and big gun.

That couldn't be – too easy – but Jim went to the rear door to be sure. The scary man didn't look so scary up close, nor did he resemble Micky Owens. But it *could* be Owens – Jim's mental picture of Owens had grown hazy, a delayed reaction to the trauma of the kidnapping perhaps.

"Excuse me," Jim said purposely brushing against the man on his way out the door, causing the man to angrily mutter, "got a problem?" but in retrospect more likely was, "not a problem."

He was stunned to find that his hand was shaking when he unlocked the front door to his house. Easy there, big fella, he muttered to himself. All the times scary dudes testified on the witness stand a scant few feet from him, insisting that no way did they murder that man, woman, or child, and he didn't remember his hand ever shaking. What was going on? Why had Aaron Winters's kidnapping rattled him so? Because he saw it happen? Because he could identify with Aaron? None of the above? Calm down, Jim, he told himself.

First thing he did was pour himself a glass of wine and take it into the living room. Second thing he did was call Enrique Montgomery at the FBI. Enrique wasn't in his office. Jim left a message.

Enrique didn't call back until the end of the day. By then, Jim had regained most of his composure. What he said to Enrique was, "Any news about Aaron Winters?" instead of what he had planned to say, "I think I'm losing my grip."

"Not a word. You?"

"I thought I saw his kidnapper on the #1 bus today, but decided afterwards I was hallucinating."

"What made you think it was Owens?"

"A slight resemblance, but I'm seeing kidnappers everywhere since I witnessed the real deal."

"A kidnapping in broad daylight from a crowded coffee shop will not go unsolved, Jim. Every police, sheriff's, and FBI office has Owens's picture. Your role will come when he's on trial and you are on the witness stand. Until then, take a deep breath. Relax."

"Repeat that word? Relax? Could you define that for me?"

"Okay, chill. Do you prefer that?"

"Chill. Yes, I think of myself as very chill."

"You are full of the proverbial shit."

"No, I'm sitting in my living room drinking a glass of half-bad Chinon. I am chill personified."

"Seriously, Jim. Everything okay?"

"It is now. I was flailing before you called. Thanks, Enrique. I'll speak highly of you when the press digs up dirt in your past."

"I'm trying to remember why I like you."

"Who doesn't?"

"Every lawyer who ever appeared in your court."

"With that exception."

"So are you off the ledge? Whatever ledge you were on? Can I go now?"

"Yes, you may. And you go with my thanks.'

"Jim, if we learn anything new about the Winters's kidnapping, you can rest assured I will tell you. Until then, leave it to us."

4

Jim felt rejuvenated in the morning. A heart-to-heart with the FBI and a good night's sleep were all it took. A little digging after breakfast, and Jim located Aaron Winters's senior adviser at MIT, Nelson Cook. Cook's office was off the Infinite Corridor in the building with the dome beloved by MIT student pranksters.

Cook seemed too young to advise anybody. He had soft eyes and a deep frown.

"Welcome to my spacious office, Judge Randall." Cook swept his arm in a truncated arc. "Your name has made its way around the campus. You were a judge for a long time, were you not?"

"Twenty-one years."

"I've been at MIT fourteen. I teach introductory quantum mechanics and I advise a handful of seniors. Aaron Winters was one of them. A shame what happened to him. I'm told you saw it happen."

"Yes, I did. So I have a personal interest in his case. What can you tell me about him?"

"Very intense young man, like most MIT students. I didn't know him well enough to know what was driving him, but based on several comments he made in our mentoring meetings, I sensed a fairly typical father-son conflict, greatly intensified by the father being an eminence on the MIT campus. Aaron knows what he wants in his life, but doesn't quite have the nerve to turn his back on his dad."

"Good kid?"

"Terrific kid. Sullen at times, but never cruel. Went out of his way to avoid hurting people."

"Why would anyone want to kidnap him?"

"That's what I've been trying to figure out. My initial instinct was that it was an elaborate prank – MIT students are notorious pranksters – but as time has passed and the prank hasn't been revealed, that seems unlikely. Some sort of warning? I don't know."

"That seems improbable," Jim said.

"I agree. I confess I'm at a loss and I hate feeling at a loss. I'd rather be wrong than at a loss."

"I've met his father. I can see why Aaron feared his wrath."

"Edgar Winters is a legend around here. If MIT's Great Dome had faces carved on it like Mount Rushmore, Professor Winters's face would be one of them."

"He's that renowned, huh?"

"Renowned and unloved." Cook fell silent to reboot. "Do not quote me, but Professor Winters doesn't know the meaning of mercy. He doesn't scream, doesn't yell, just ruthlessly pummels his opponents into submission, one irrefutable argument at a time."

"Professor Winters was the reason I got involved in this case. Aaron was about to throw his future away, according to his father," Jim said.

"I didn't see that. Aaron was doing well in school, maybe a slight drop-off in the quality of his work as he approached graduation, but his work was at a high level anyway, so a slight drop-off didn't amount to a danger sign."

"Did Aaron confide any change of plans to you?"

"Change of plans? Let me think. I know he was torn about following his fiancée to Burlington, but the University of Vermont is a good school, if he chooses to get his doctorate there."

"Ex-fiancée. They ended their engagement."

"I didn't know that. His father must have been pleased to learn that."

"Why do you say that?"

"Edgar is an MIT man all the way, so there must have been consternation about the prospect of his son continuing his studies at the University of Vermont."

"You've been very helpful. May I contact you again if I have more questions?"

"Of course."

Jim rose. "Thanks for your time."

"I hope Aaron is okay and that you catch the bastard who did this."

Jim walked up Mass Ave after he left Cook's office. A gleaming new coffee shop with giant windows had opened along the way to Central Square, and Jim stopped for a cup of coffee. How strange to sit in a well-lit coffee shop with picture windows when he was used to the small windows and dull light of The Long Gone. Jim felt on display.

He half-watched the heavy traffic on Mass Ave and thought to himself that Aaron's kidnapping was to the ordinary kidnapping as quantum physics was to Newtonian physics. Open your mind, Jim; abandon the straight-line logic of 'if A= B, and B=C, then A=C.' Try rolling the alphabet like dice and seeing what happens.

The coffee was good but not up to Long Gone standards.

He walked the rest of the way home, only pausing to text Ernie Farrell, his computer guru. Jim did not speak computer, so he often turned to Ernie for help when investigating a crime:

> Please see what you can find for me on
> Professor Edgar Winters of MIT. He's the dad
> of the kidnapped student.

Ernie replied before dinner:

> Widely considered a genius. Recipient of
> numerous awards. Scuttlebutt has him
> next in line for a Nobel. Drops out of sight
> periodically. Rumor has it that he checks
> himself into McLean Mental Hospital to
> unstick his brain the way some people
> periodically check themselves into spas.
> Nobody likes him.

Jim climbed to his study. Genius father with mental problems, promising son with low self-esteem. Synergy or sparks?

Jim must have fallen asleep in his study. He had no memory of doing so and was surprised when Pat woke him. "I must have fallen asleep," he said. "How did you get in?"

"I used my key."

Jim struggled upright. "Of course. I'm groggy."

She examined him closely. "Are you okay?"

"Fine."

"Get up slowly."

"I'm fine, Pat."

"I don't want you to fall."

He wobbled as he got up. "See? I'm fine."

"Come downstairs and tell me about your day."

Jim felt solid sitting at his kitchen table looking out his back window at his garage. Pat brought him a glass of wine. "Now tell me about your meeting with Nelson Cook."

"Thanks." Jim sipped the wine. "Quintessential nerd with more self-awareness than most, which is to say, not much. I asked him about Edgar Winters. Professor Winters is apparently a fearsome presence around MIT. Cook said his face belongs on MIT's Mount Rushmore. I get the sense that Aaron and his father were oil and water."

"Actively hostile to each other?"

"Cook wouldn't go that far, but I got the sense they didn't have much in common except last names and high intellects. Aaron was struggling to find his place in the world, which isn't unusual at that age, but having a father who won't give an inch undoubtedly made it harder. Being kidnapped took matters out of Aaron's hands, which I can imagine almost being a relief for Aaron." Jim stirred. "I'm getting hungry. What are we going to do for dinner?"

"What's in your refrigerator?"

"I have no idea, probably nothing."

"Then we have two options, as far as I can see."

"I can guess. Go out or take out."

Pat poked Jim's shoulder. "Well done. Which will it be?"

*

Nothing more about the kidnapping had appeared in the pages of the *Boston Globe* for days when Jim arranged to meet with Sasha Cohen. Sasha Cohen had been a reporter for an alternative weekly when Jim first met her, now she wrote for the *Globe*. They occasionally gave each other tips on cases. He found her smart, discreet, sensitive to the nuances of a crime; someone who kept her word when Jim declared something off the record. He liked working with her.

To say that Sasha waltzed into The Long Gone would not be a figure of speech because her slight build and short height made her seem to dance on air when she was in a hurry. She started talking as soon as she sat down.

"The *Globe* received an anonymous tip that someone fitting the description of Aaron Winters was spotted in the Cambridgeside Galleria last night. The caller wouldn't stay on the line, so we couldn't get details. This is the first tip we've received since the initial flurry."

"If Aaron has escaped his captor, why would he go shopping?"

"That's what we wondered. My guess is that this is another false lead, but I thought you'd like to know. Have you made any progress?"

"Not much. Aaron and his father didn't get along, but if every son who didn't get along with his father disappeared, we'd have a lot more missing persons."

"And Micky Owens hasn't turned up yet. Maybe he and Aaron were abducted by aliens."

Sasha rarely displayed whimsey, so it took Jim a few seconds to respond in kind. "Which would make them the victims of an interplanetary crime."

Sasha looked at Jim more closely than usual. "Nope, whimsey's not for you, Jim."

"Then may I vent to you?"

Sasha looked concerned. "Of course. Is something wrong?"

"I usually get depressed at some point in every investigation, but I'm depressed earlier than usual in this one. That troubles me."

"Everything okay with you and Pat?"

"Fine."

"Then is it something about this case?"

"It has something to do with Aaron Winters. Even though I was with him for only a short time, he has stuck in my mind. There was something about him..."

Sasha's phone pinged. She dug it out of her pocket, read the text, and without a word handed the phone to Jim.

"What is it?" he asked.

"Take a look."

Body Of Suspected Kidnapper

Found In Mystic River

The body of Micky Owens, suspected kidnapper of MIT student Aaron Winters, was spotted early this morning floating in the Mystic River. Given the condition of the body and where it was found, the police speculate that Owens leapt to his death from the Tobin Bridge shortly after the kidnapping.

5

Jim reached Enrique Montgomery on the phone.

"I've only got a minute, Jim."

"I'll be quick. I just read that Micky Owens's body was found. What can you tell me?"

"Micky Owens was in the terminal stages of cancer. Probably in a great deal of pain. We think he pulled off one last score, then killed himself to end the pain. We think whoever hired him to kidnap Aaron knew he planned to end his life, but who hired him is still a mystery to us and to the DA. The Mayor is furious at us for knowing so little. We've found Micky Owens's body, but we haven't found Aaron Winters. We don't even know if he is alive or dead. We look like fools, according to the mayor's office. I have to cut this short, Jim. I'm about to receive a tongue-lashing from said Mayor."

"While you're getting a tongue-lashing, I'm going to call Edgar Winters again. He's not telling us everything he knows and this morning's news may loosen his tongue."

Edgar Winters beat Jim to it. He called Jim almost immediately after Jim got off the phone with Enrique. He was angry. "Where is my son?" he demanded "No one is telling me anything."

"All I know is that both federal and state law enforcement are looking for him as we speak."

"Incompetents, all of you."

"Edgar, I believe you know more than you've told us. If you want to find your son, you'll tell us everything you know, and I mean everything."

Professor Winters sounded indignant. "But I've told you everything I know." Pause. "Fine, it's a waste of time, but let's meet. Do you know a bar called Dark Matter?"

"I've heard of it."

"Between Kendall and Harvard Squares."

"I'll find it."

Dark Matter was one part dive bar, one part nerd bar and one part Nobel Prize winners-to-be bar. Winters and Jim sat side-by-side at the Pi-shaped bar.

Jim said, "Knowing that your son's kidnapper can no longer tell us where your son is must be excruciating."

"Believe me, it is." Winters didn't raise his head from his whiskey glass.

"So we have to find your son. Has anything you haven't told us come to your mind? Anything you might have overlooked, anything he said, anything he did?"

Winters lifted his head to look at Jim. "I told the FBI, the DA, the police, everything I know. There's nothing I haven't told the authorities. What about you? You were the last person to see Aaron alive."

"Yes, but I was with him for only a few minutes and I'm only an amateur detective."

"Which is good. You approach puzzles with an open mind. Eventually you'll become jaded and leap to conclusions. I tell my students, retain the curiosity of a child. The discovery of the kidnapper's body without finding my son convinces me that the authorities are being played for fools. Eventually they'll learn that my son's kidnapping was part of an elaborate plot to beat me to the holy grail."

"Excuse me? The holy grail?"

"Updating Einstein to include what we've learned from quantum mechanics."

"Let me get this straight. Your son was kidnapped to prevent you from solving a physics problem?"

"Don't you understand? Whoever solves the puzzle first will surely win the Nobel Prize."

"I confess I don't see how your son's kidnapping ties into your chances for the Nobel."

Professor Winters grew animated. "To *distract* me. To keep me from my work! For God's sake, man, wake up!"

In his years as a judge, Jim had learned not to be surprised by human nature, but Professor Winters's self-absorption was extreme. Retain the curiosity of a child, fine, but Winters had also retained the 'me, me, me!' immaturity of a child. Jim had started this case by wishing he knew more self-critical men, but instead had stumbled upon one of the most self-absorbed men he had ever met.

Winters was still heated. "Scientists are among the most competitive people on earth, Judge. Some rival of mine hired Micky Owens to kidnap my son. Mark my words."

*

When Jim was stuck in a case, appalled by human nature, or just plain tired, his default remedy was to go to his Vermont house. He asked Pat if she wanted to come.

"How long are you planning to stay?"

"A few days at most."

"Jim, I think you need time alone."

Jim's house was a few miles north of Brattleboro. He and his late wife had bought it as a getaway when both were working in Montpelier. The house perched just below the top of a hill overlooking the Connecticut River, the border between Vermont and New Hampshire. Jim loved how the light played with the river, highlighting it, hiding it, digging it deeper into its valley. He always went to his living room window to check the river when he first got to his house. This trip the light seemed to dull the river, smudge it.

Staring at the valley, Jim called Pat. "Hi, I made it."

"Good. How's the valley?" She knew his habits.

"The valley is sulking."

"Then you'll have company."

"I don't sulk, I brood."

"What are you going to do for dinner?"

"Don't rush me."

"Go down to the village store and bring back some of their lasagna. You like their lasagna."

"I may do that."

"Did you have any insights into the case as you were driving up?"

"None. A big disappointment."

"Hearing your voice makes me wish I had come up with you."

"Let that be a lesson."

Jim had lasagna for dinner. He thought it was his idea.

Jim stayed two days. As always it was good to get away, but it gave him no insights as to where to find Aaron, or whether he was alive. If he was but his kidnapper was now dead, who was holding him hostage? And given that no ransom demand had been made, why was he kidnapped and who was behind it? Aaron's father, as seemed likely?

He drove home empty-handed and empty-headed, which meant he arrived home ornery. He called Pat to tell her he was home but that she should stay away from him that night for her own good.

"Bunk. I'm coming over. Unless you don't want me."

"I'd love to have you here, but I'm not feeling judicious."

"You don't frighten me, Jim. That probably disappoints you, but it's true."

It was good to see her. She brought dignity into whatever room she entered. She was carrying a bag of groceries. "I stopped and got takeout."

"Something I like?"

"Not a chance. But you will eat it because it's good for you, and because I bought it."

"I'll open a bottle of the wine I save for special occasions, and we'll celebrate an everyday dinner together. The best kind."

After a dinner of supermarket roast chicken and green salad, they sat in Jim's living room, Pat reading, Jim trying to connect the dots of Aaron Winters's kidnapping now that his kidnapper was dead. Maybe no one was holding Aaron hostage. Maybe he was alive and well, enjoying his newfound freedom from his father's expectations. Jim could imagine Aaron saying, "Simmer down, people, this is the first time in my life I've felt free of my father's withering gaze, I'll come out of hiding when I'm good and ready. In the meantime, let me breathe freely for a few days, please. Thank you very much."

Jim could partially identify with Aaron's frustration, even though their fathers were nothing alike. Jim's dad had been an emotionally inaccessible man with a quick temper. He didn't seem to know how to deal with a son. Jim had come to terms with his father by realizing that his father had done the best he could, but reaching that point had taken Jim years.

"Jim, I'm trying to talk to you. Can you hear me?"

"Of course I can."

It was Pat, reading in the chair next to his. "You were lost to this world. Where were you?"

"Back in my childhood, where I rarely go."

"For a moment, I was worried you were having a stroke."

"No, I am *not* having a stroke."

"Relax, Jim. I'm on your side. Literally."

"Of course. I'm sorry."

"Old wounds are the worst."

"I was comparing Edgar Winters to my father. Dad was not the father I wished for, but he did the best he could. Edgar Winters is another matter. Edgar Winters is, pardon the expression, an asshole with no redeeming qualities, so I can imagine Aaron resorting to extremes to punish him, or conversely, to make his father appreciate him."

"By having himself kidnapped?"

"It's conceivable."

"But hard to imagine for a super-smart young man with a brilliant future before him."

"Be gentle, I'm just trying ideas on for size. And now I'm done for the night." Jim stood and stretched. "I'm going to bed. Coming?"

"When I finish the chapter I'm reading."

He climbed the stairs; his Cambridge townhouse had stairs, lots of stairs. Aaron Winters, Aaron Winters, come out wherever you are, he chanted with each step.

*

Time to update Ted.

The Ipsa Loquitur Happy Hour was a grim affair. Litigators crowding the bar and lowering their swords, without raising their spirits. Jim arrived before Ted, Ted a few minutes later.

Ted took the last stool. "How goes it?" he said, signaling the bartender for a beer.

"I'd feel a lot better if I knew whether Aaron Winters is still alive. Do you have any new leads?" Jim asked.

"We do not and neither do the feds. The case will remain open, but for now, it is not our top priority."

"I was afraid you'd say that."

"What about you? Any new insights?"

"Nothing solid, only a hunch that this is more a father-son thing than your usual case of kidnapping."

"There is one new item. We have confirmed that Micky Owens's body entered the water shortly after the kidnapping. Hard to tell exactly when because of the damage to the body caused by immersion in the water, but the estimate is the day of the kidnapping."

"When Micky Owens snatched Aaron Winters at gunpoint from The Long Gone, Owens looked to be in bad physical shape. Was an autopsy done on the body?"

"Yes. Cause of death was drowning, accompanied by blunt force injuries consistent with a body hitting water at high speeds. State police have not been able to locate any witnesses who saw Owens go off the Tobin Bridge, but a car that had been reported stolen was found abandoned on the bridge. We have a witness who saw a man matching Owens's description break into the car in Mattapan earlier that evening."

"No other findings from the autopsy?"

"Owens would have died soon from natural causes. His lungs were riddled with tumors. The doc was surprised he had the strength to pull off a kidnapping."

"So kidnapping Winters was one of the last things he did."

"Maybe the very last."

"Which leads back to the question, why? Why kidnap Winters as his last act on earth?"

"I assume he was hired to do it and had some reason to need the money even though he wouldn't live to spend it."

"A reasonable assumption. But once again, why?"

Jim watched a man his age, give or take a year or two, approach a table full of women and put his arm around the shoulder of one of them. The woman didn't shake the arm off but she didn't look pleased. Jim wondered how well they knew each other. Couldn't tell.

Pay attention, Jim. Ted is asking you a question.

"Jim, do you ever miss the days when you all you had to do was rule on objections and occasionally render a verdict?"

"You know the job of a judge better than that," Jim winced.

"Okay, so a lot was riding on your acumen. Better?"

"Much. And sometimes I do miss the days when I was presented with a set of facts on which to decide, rather than having to dig up the facts myself."

"I don't want to play to your needy ego, but once in a while, I miss having you on the bench."

"Like hell you do."

"No, I do. Then I come to my senses."

Jim swallowed a chuckle. "Gotta go. I'm meeting Pat for dinner."

"How's Pat?"

"Great. She's hard at work on the second volume of her memoirs, writes the occasional op-ed or law review piece, and volunteers as a moot court judge for third-year law students at Suffolk."

"Good for her. She's top notch. Arguing a case in her courtroom was an intimidating experience, but I always came away the better for it. Say hello for me."

It was a short walk across the Charles to Pat's apartment. They ate at the bistro at the foot of Beacon Hill.

Jim liked sitting across a dinner table from Pat. Her put-together looks did not shout or preen; they had no need to. He had no defenses against them.

He reached across the table for her hand. "Do you ever wish you had children?"

"What brought that on? We're a little old for that, don't you think?"

"I don't mean you and me. I meant you and your late husband. Do you regret you and he didn't have kids"

"Sometimes yes, sometimes no, presently learning no. I think I'm too judgmental to have been a good mother. Why do you ask?"

"Because I wish I understood what it's like to be a parent. Maybe I'd understand Edgar Winters better if I did."

"From what you've told me, Edgar Winters is not your typical dad, nor is Aaron Winters your typical son."

A waiter approached. Jim scanned his menu. "What are you going to have, Pat?"

"The coq au vin. You?"

"The cod." Jim didn't like fish but knew it was good for him. He'd have ice cream for desert to make up for it.

The young waiter took their orders and their menus.

Pat said to Jim, "I have a friend you could speak to. Mary Higgins. She's a family counselor of long standing. She might be able to help you understand the dynamic between Winters the elder and Winters the son."

Curmudgeons are loathe to seek help, but Jim was only part-curmudgeon, so he made an appointment with Mary Higgins.

"Pat tells me you two served on the court together," Mary Higgins said. Her red hair was trending white and her green eyes had an intensity that was only partly softened by her ready smile.

"Yes, we did. We had a close professional relationship, but nothing more, I assure you."

Higgins held up her hand. "Let me stop you there. Even if you two ravaged each other in chambers, it's none of my business."

Jim exhaled. "Good, because we did. The bailiffs had to tell us to keep the noise down."

Higgins straightened a smile. "Pat tells me you're trying to understand a complex father-son relationship. From what she told me, you're looking at a son who has his father's brains but not his personality or his professional interests."

"Exactly."

"In most cases that wouldn't be an insurmountable barrier, but it sounds like it is in this case."

"The father is limited in what he can understand, including but not limited to, other human beings. A brilliant man who lacks the ability to relate to people."

Higgins nodded. "That's quite common, in fact."

"But the father has received so much professional praise he thinks he understands everything, including his son. Which makes getting though to him almost impossible. He's often mentioned as a candidate for the Nobel Prize."

"You'd be amazed how many of my clients have that distinction," Higgins said.

"What can you tell me to help me understand?"

"You're obviously sympathetic to the son, but I caution you to remember he is still young and lacking in life experience. Just as it is hard for the father to move past fact to feeling, the son may have the problem of getting past his feelings to fact."

"A plague on both their houses?"

"No, not quite. What I'm saying is keep an open mind and don't expect to find explanations that satisfy your own biases. Human behavior is inexplicable, irrational and self-defeating. I'd be on the lookout for self-defeating behavior on the part of the son. The son may seek a way out of his dilemma that only makes it worse."

"Might that include suicide?"

"I wouldn't go that far, but if the son wanted his father's attention badly enough, I can see him going to extremes."

"If so, he has failed. His father is as self-absorbed as ever."

Jim reported to Pat that evening over dinner in his kitchen. "Your friend Mary Higgins was helpful. How long have you known her?"

"I sought her advice when my late husband and I were having marriage trouble, just before his death. She pointed out to me that his illness was changing his behavior, and that I should have more patience. She was right."

"Patience. Good advice for amateur sleuths and lay-people alike."

"Isn't an amateur sleuth a layperson by definition?"

"Did I ever tell you that you are a pain in the ass?"

"No, because you are too dignified to speak like that."

*

Time for another visit to Concord State Prison and Skip Lockhardt. Jim cursed the traffic on Route 2. Even in early afternoon, the traffic moved like a centipede. By the time he reached the prison, his head was about to explode.

Lockhardt had aged since Jim's last visit. The flashes of anger that had kept his eyes from seeming dead had faded to feeble sparks, his skin seemed even more cadaverous.

"How are you?" Jim said in the visiting room

"What a dumb question. Look at me. Why did you want to see me again? I told you everything I know."

"I missed your bubbly personality."

"Okay, we're even. So ask your questions, then leave me alone."

"Last time you said Micky Owens was nuts. Talk more about that."

"Bonkers, unbalanced. One minute calculating and shrewd, the next off-the-wall. I gave up trying to decipher him."

"Rants and raves?"

"Plus insults and threats. Then docile and friendly. Like I say, off the wall."

"Did Micky ever mention the name Aaron Winters?"

"Aaron Winters? The kid he kidnapped?"

"Yes."

"Micky never mentioned the kid's name. You don't mean Edgar Winters, do you?"

"Micky talked about Edgar Winters?"

"More than once. Micky fancied himself a brain. He wrote a fan letter to Edgar Winters saying something like, reading your book on space-time takes my mind off where I am. Something like that, I don't remember the exact wording. He bragged about his correspondence with Professor Winters all the time."

"Professor Winters replied to Micky's letter?"

"According to Micky, yes."

"Did you ever see the letters?"

"Micky's letters, but not Professor Winters's. Do you think he made them up to impress me?"

"No, I think he was telling you the truth. I'm just curious about what Winters might have said."

"Is it true that Micky jumped off the Tobin Bridge?"

"Jumped is the official verdict. Jumped or dumped, he ended up in the river."

"I'd put my money on jumped."

"Why?"

"Because Micky was dying. He hated waiting for the cancer to kill him. He tried killing himself in prison but the guards caught him. Took matters into his own hands once he got out is my guess. Poor Micky. It's bad enough to be nuts, but then to be at the mercy of something like cancer." Lockhardt shook his head. "Did I mention that I'm not in very good shape myself? I may not be around much longer. What's it like out there these days? Is the world as crazy as it sounds?"

"Yes. Things are falling apart, the center cannot hold."

"Yeats, correct?"

"Yes. I'm surprised."

"That I know how to read? Not a lot to do in here except read or fight. Shame on you."

"I accept your verdict. Shame on me."

"But the world is crazy?"

"We seem to be going through a period of realignment, the old ways no longer work and we are fighting about what the new ways will be."

"So I'm not missing much by being inside?"

"I wouldn't go that far."

"I like talking to you, Judge. Ignore what I said earlier about leaving me alone. Come anytime."

6

For most of its 825 feet, MIT's Infinite Corridor resembles a long utility corridor in the basement of an aging office building. There is nothing inspiring about it except its length. But twice a year, the sun briefly shines the entire length of the corridor, an event heralded by student and faculty alike. It was raining when Jim paid another visit to Edgar Winters, so Jim took the Infinite Corridor to building E73. You'd think he'd know the way by now, but only when he came within sight of Winters's office was he sure he had reached his destination. Winters was expecting, if not delighted, to see him.

"You are dogged, I'll give you that." Winters received Jim leaning back in a wooden chair, his fingertips tapping each other in an urgent private rhythm.

"As a scientist, you should appreciate doggedness."

"I do, oh, I do. That's why I agreed to meet with you again. What is this, the fourth time?"

"Third, but I'm not counting. Anyway, I won't take up much of your time. I have learned that Micky Owens, your son's kidnapper, wrote you a fan letter. And that you corresponded with him. Why didn't you tell me?"

"Because I knew it would give the wrong impression, which is why I didn't tell the police either. Since you will surely ask, I'll show you the one letter I saved. I didn't save the entire correspondence, because his neediness became embarrassing. Do you want to see what I've got?"

"That's why I'm here."

Winters picked a letter from his desk drawer and handed it to Jim.

It was indeed a fan letter, not a ransom note. No warnings, no threats, or demands for money. Confined in prison, Micky Owens had sought relief in strange worlds of the mind, including the world of quantum mechanics. Quantum mechanics was Micky Owens's get-out-of-jail card.

> I only understand a little of what you write,
> but it sets my mind to dreaming here
> in my cell, and for that, I thank you.

Jim looked up from the letter.

"Do you see why I replied?" Owens said.

"Yes, but why don't you tell me."

"Because it originated from inside a prison cell and came from a man who obviously didn't understand my work. That my work could touch such a man intrigued me."

"So you wrote back. What happened then?"

"We exchanged letters, and then I stopped hearing from him. I don't know why. He never gave a hint he would later kidnap my son, but I thought the police would assume I was somehow involved if they saw his letters, so I threw the rest of them away. I couldn't bear to throw this one away for the reason I explained."

"You must admit it looks suspicious, throwing away the letters of the man who kidnapped your son."

"I know how it looks, but there was nothing in the letters to suggest what he was about to do."

Jim left Edgar Winters's office no closer to understanding than before. Oh, for a simple set of facts! Oh, for a cookie-cutter crime! Have pity on amateur detectives, oh minor deity of unsolved mysteries! When he stumbled from the Infinite Corridor into the noise and pollution of Mass Ave, he felt dazed. In the world of Newtonian physics, the rain had stopped and mist rose off the asphalt. In the world of quantum mechanics, a released con had kidnapped a young man, then jumped off a bridge. A #1 bus slalomed through a puddle as it pulled to the curb, spraying Jim with gutter water.

At least Jim now had a plausible idea of how Micky Owens had learned of Aaron Winters: Edgar Winters must have mentioned Aaron in one of his letters to Owens. Was kidnapping the son a twisted way for Owens to inhabit the professor's world? Or was there a more conventional motive: ransom?

Jim stayed at Pat's that night. "I'm hopelessly out of my depth," Jim complained as they read in bed.

"As you endlessly say, start with the simplest explanation, then add complexity as needed. I'll bet there's a simple, which is not to say a rational, explanation. I'll bet the kidnapping made perfect sense to whoever planned it."

"What are you reading?" Jim asked.

"*To The Lighthouse*. I read it in college and want to see how I have changed."

"I tried to read that years ago but gave up."

"Don't give up on Aaron Winters. He needs you." Pat switched off her light. "Goodnight, Jim."

Jim switched off his light and tried to sleep.

"Do you think Aaron is still alive?" Jim asked after a few minutes.

"I was almost asleep."

"Sorry."

"Yes, I do, I think Aaron's still alive."

"On a scale of one to ten, how certain are you?"

"Seven. Now let me sleep."

Jim awoke the next morning thinking that the best hope of locating Aaron Winters, if he was still alive, lay through Skip Lockhardt. Micky Owens might have said something to him that Lockhardt didn't think relevant until prodded by Jim. 'Come back anytime,' he had said, so after breakfast Jim drove again to the prison.

Bad timing. The traffic around the Concord rotary was stop and stop. If an escaped prisoner tried to flee by car, they'd only get as far as the rotary where they'd have to ditch the car and flee on foot.

The guards were getting used to the sight of a former judge by the name of Randall visiting their prison to see a scumbag by the name of Lockhardt. Lockhardt was brought to the visitor's room after Jim's arrival.

Lockhardt shuffled into the visitor's room as if shackled, dragging one leg behind the other. Jim hadn't noticed his walk before.

"You said to come back anytime."

"And here you are," Lockhardt said when seated. "I'm feeling old today. Cheer me up."

"Tell me something I don't already know about Micky Owens."

"That doesn't cheer me up."

"And when you do, I'll lavish you with praise. That ought to do the trick."

"I'm afraid you'll be disappointed. I've already told you everything I know."

"I'm looking for ordinary things, things you might not think to mention. Start with anything Owens said about his birthplace."

"Someplace in Indiana."

"Good. Keep going. What did his parents do?"

"No idea. To hear him talk, he didn't have parents."

"Siblings?"

"A sister, come to think of it. But I don't remember her name."

"Think hard."

Lockhardt shook his head. "Not a chance I'll remember."

"Do you remember if her last name was the same as his?"

"I think so. No, it wasn't, it was something like Conrad."

"Good. Very good."

Lockhardt lit up. "Yes, that's it! Her last name is Conrad, first name Mavis. Mavis Conrad. Yes, that's it!"

"Excellent. Do you know where she lives?"

"It's starting to come back! She lives in North Dakota, somewhere in North Dakota, working with Native Americans. I'm proud of myself for remembering."

*

Locating Mavis Conrad wasn't easy. It took the combined efforts of Ernie Farrell, Enrique Montgomery, and most importantly, a friend of Enrique's who worked at the Bureau of Indian Affairs. Mavis Conrad had dropped off the grid to bond with the Spirit Creek Nation, taking the spiritual name of Running Rain Water and becoming a leader in the campaign to prevent violence against Native American women.

To arrange a phone call with her took several days. Enrique's friend provided the name of someone she knew in the Spirit Creek Nation who knew Mavis. And that led to Mavis agreeing to a phone call.

"But she doesn't want you to disrespect her new life. Do you promise?"

"Absolutely," Jim answered. "Tell her I'm a retired judge and shall respect her life and her privacy."

At the agreed-upon time, Mavis came on the phone.

"Hello?"

"Hello, this is Judge Randall. Thank you for talking to me. What would you like me to call you?"

"Mavis is fine." She sounded hesitant, unsure. Jim couldn't tell her age from her voice.

"Let me explain why I'm calling. Since I retired from the bench, I have become a self-appointed amateur detective. I have no official role and you have no obligation to speak to me. You can hang up at any moment and you won't be in trouble. Okay?"

Again, hesitant. "Okay."

"I'm very sorry about the loss of your brother. I was in the coffee shop when he kidnapped young Aaron Winters. It's not everyday I witness a kidnapping, and it left an indelible impression. Since then, I have been trying to learn if Aaron Winters is still alive. Are you with me so far?"

Mavis's voice grew stronger. "Yes, I live a cloistered life in many ways, but news does reach me, and I knew what my brother had done. We had not spoken in years, but I was aware he had been in and out of prison. Whenever I reached out to him, he brushed me aside. I stopped trying years ago."

"Are you his only living relative?"

"Me and his daughter."

"He had a daughter?"

"Yes. Abigail. He had little to do with her after she was born, and he barely knew the mother. Micky and the mother didn't stay together. I was a teenager living with a foster family and Micky was in his twenties living on his own. He and I were still on speaking terms then, and one day – out of the blue – he told me he was going to have a child. He didn't sound happy about it. It was around then that Micky went to jail for the first time. He held up a convenience store."

"Do you know where Abigail is now?"

"No. She must be in her thirties, but I have no way of knowing where she is."

"Do you happen to know her last name? Is it Owens?"

"I would doubt it. Probably her mother's last name, which I don't know." Mavis fell silent. Jim let her have her silence. When she spoke, it was to say, "Do you know how surreal our conversation sounds to me? I am taking this call in the main lodge of the Spirit Creek Nation. Out the window I see fields that go on forever, and you and I are talking about a brother I hardly knew, his daughter who I never met, and a kidnapping in a coffee shop."

"I didn't mean to upset you."

"Not upset, startled. I forget how throughly I removed myself from my brother's world. Different universes, different measures of time. Eternity versus years. Goodbye, Judge Randall. I wish you luck in your quest, but please respect me in mine, and do not contact me again."

"I won't, if that's what you want, but may I ask why?"

"I prefer to stay in eternity. Goodbye, Judge. Good luck."

Jim was disoriented when the call ended. He looked out the window to orient himself; instead of fields stretching to eternity, he saw multi-family houses on a city street in Cambridge, where egos duke it out and reputations have shelf lives of nano-seconds.

Abigail. A woman in her thirties. Last name and location unknown. How to find her?

To start, Jim met with Ernie Farrell, master of all things digital, and asked him to do his magic.

"I can't do magic when all I have is a first name."

"Her father is Micky Owens, the deceased suspect in the kidnapping of Aaron Winters."

"Okay, now we're getting somewhere. I'll get back to you."

Next, Jim emailed Ted Conover. "Can you check prison records for information on Micky Owens's daughter? First name is Abigail, last name and location unknown.."

Ted's reply: "Micky had a daughter?"

"That was my reaction. Yes, he had a daughter. And an estranged sister named Mavis who is living with the Spirit Creek Nation in North Dakota."

"This gets stranger and stranger. Still no sign of Aaron Winters, I assume?"

"Not unless you guys have found him."

"Nope. Off our radar."

Who put Micky Owens up to kidnapping Aaron Winters? It hadn't been Owens's idea, Jim was sure. To kidnap someone in broad daylight, then wind up dead in the Mystic River, is not the mark of a lone wolf. Somebody put him up to it.

Neither Ted nor Ernie found any info on Abigail, last name unknown. Let the authorities handle this, Jim, he told himself. Don't be stubborn. It's okay to strike out once in a while.

He spent the next week at Pat's, a longer stretch than usual. As when he had stayed there more than a few days in the past, she eventually sent unmistakable signals that she needed time alone. He didn't take offense then or now because an idea was brewing in his mind.

"I need to go up to Burlington again," he told Pat.

"To see Aaron Winters's fiancée?"

"Ex-fiancée. Yes."

"I think I'll stay here."

"Are you angry?"

"Not at all. I just think it's a colossal waste of time, and I've got work to do."

The three and a half hours to Burlington felt long without Pat. He thought of stopping at his Brattleboro house for the night but decided against it. Stick to your plan. Don't be a wuss.

He was exhausted by the time he arrived in Burlington. He found a room at the cheapest hotel he could find and lay down to take a nap. He wasn't due to meet Melanie Johnson until dinner time.

The restaurant where they were to meet was on the first corner of the pedestrian street. It specialized in kebabs. Jim didn't understand kebabs, didn't know how to eat them, but was willing to eat anywhere Melanie wanted.

She looked different than he remembered, although he didn't remember her appearance well. He accurately remembered her as being short, but her face was rounder than he remembered and her eyes more unforgiving. Her eyes didn't go with her face. Her face looked jolly or at least good natured, while her eyes said cut the crap. To his surprise, he felt a little intimidated; usually when he questioned people, it was the other way around.

He began his questioning light-heartedly. Disarm her, feel her out.

"I've never understood kebabs. How do you eat them?"

She looked at him. "Are you serious?"

"I am. I'm not a foodie."

"It doesn't take a foodie to know how to eat a kebab. You slide 'em off the skewer and eat them like any other kind of food."

"You don't eat them on the skewer?"

"Come on, get serious. You didn't drive three hours to talk about kebabs."

"Three and a half hours."

She examined his face. "Okay, I get it. Soften me up with a little light-hearted shit, then accuse me of being an accomplice to Aaron's disappearance."

"Are you?"

"An accomplice? I am laughing. Ha ha. See?"

"Do you want wine?"

"I'll stick with beer. Goes better with kebabs."

"This dinner's on me," Jim said. "So spend freely. I'm grateful you agreed to see me again."

"Okay, we're back to square go. What do you want to know that I didn't tell you before?"

"Have you heard from Aaron?"

"Is he still alive?"

"You tell me."

"You're the detective. How should I know?"

"I'd think you'd be the first person he'd contact. Has he?"

"You're out of your mind."

"Let me tell you why I ask. Most people being kidnapped at gunpoint would be visibly afraid, if not panicked. Aaron seemed more annoyed than afraid, as if things weren't going according to plan, as opposed to, 'Oh my God, what's happening?' That's just my interpretation and may be way off base, but my guess is that Aaron knew what was coming."

Melanie didn't react the way a person who had no knowledge of what Jim was talking about would react, she deflected as if Jim had touched a nerve. "I think you're being ridiculous. You may have been a good judge but you're a lousy detective and...and...," her face collapsed as if she were about to sob, "...and I resent your insinuation that I knew he'd be kidnapped."

"I did not suggest you knew in advance, I suggested Aaron knew. And if he is alive, I imagine you'd be the first person he would contact. You and he had been close for several years in college, and until very recently, had been planning to marry."

"So?"

"So I think you know whether he is alive."

The unctuous waiter appeared. "Ready to order?"

Melanie shot to her feet. "I changed my mind, I'm not staying. The judge will have a kebab." And Melanie stormed out of the restaurant.

"Sir?" the waiter said.

"I'm leaving too. Here's a little for your trouble." Jim stuffed a ten-dollar bill in the waiter's hand and walked out to a sunset over Lake Champlain. On the sidewalk, he texted Ted Conover.

> I'm in Burlington and just met with Melanie
> Johnson. I have a strong suspicion that
> Aaron Winters is alive. I'll tell you
> more when I get home tomorrow.

In his younger days, Jim would have driven the three and a half hours home in the dark, no problem, but he was no longer young and his nighttime vision wasn't as good as it used to be, so he stayed in Burlington overnight. He would drive home first thing in the morning.

A text from Ted was awaiting when he awoke.

> **Aaron Winters is alive? I await your reasoning.**

Jim:

> **I'm heading home now.**
> **I'll come straight to your office.**

He had three and a half hours to come up with a reason convincing enough to persuade a seasoned pro like Ted. All Jim had now was a hunch based on Melanie storming out of the restaurant – Ted would listen respectfully to his hunch, but wouldn't buy it. By the time Jim arrived home, he had refined his three kidnapping theories to pass muster with Ted.

> 1) Micky Owens kidnapped Aaron Winters for ransom, then something went wrong, and he jumped off the Tobin Bridge to avoid going back to prison.

> 2) Edgar Winters paid Micky Owens to kidnap Aaron to scare Aaron into staying on his father's preferred path. Hadn't Aaron started to say "Tell Dad..." when Micky Owens shut him up?

> 3) Aaron staged his own kidnapping to scare his father into leaving him alone.

Well, that narrows it down, Jim murmured as he got out of his car in Cambridge. Jim had originally thought that option #1 explained the kidnapping, but enough time had passed without a ransom demand that Jim now considered that less likely. Option #3 was unlikely to achieve its goal given how little Edgar cared for his son ("Me? Scared because my son's missing? You have to be kidding!"), and Aaron was smart enough to know that. Which left option # 2. It seemed like something Edgar Winters would do.

7

"I vote for none of the above," Ted said in his office.

As Ted Conover spoke, he paced from his desk to his window. How many times had Jim seen Ted pace to his window and back? It never seemed to matter to Ted what he saw out the window, it was the pacing and peering that mattered. Jim did the same thing whenever he got to his Vermont house, so he could identify.

Ted turned from the window. "If Aaron was kidnapped for ransom, and his kidnapper is dead, why hasn't Aaron contacted anyone?"

"Maybe he can't."

"Are you saying he's being held captive?"

"Or he's dead. And the fact we don't know he's contacted anyone doesn't mean he hasn't."

"His father?"

"His father would be the last person Aaron would contact."

"Then who?"

"Melanie Johnson."

"Didn't you tell me that she and Aaron broke off heir engagement?"

"Yes, but that doesn't mean they're not in touch. When I raised the subject with Melanie at dinner last night, she lost her composure and stalked from the restaurant. Her phone records would show whether Aaron's been in touch with her."

"We have no basis to request a subpoena of her phone records, you know that."

"I know that."

"Not enough evidence. In fact, no evidence."

"You don't have to rub it in."

Ted grimaced. "You bastard, do you know how many times you turned down subpoena requests from my office?"

"Too many to count."

"So I have every right to rub it in. To make up for it, the next time we meet at Ipsa Loquitor, I'll buy you a glass of their house red."

"I don't drink swill."

Ted grinned. "I know."

Pat's apartment was an easy walk across the Charles from Ted's office. He opened the door with his key.

"Pat?" he called once he was inside. Pat had warned him that she might not be home when he arrived. He settled down to wait.

He was half-dozing when he heard Pat's key in the door.

He pushed himself upright and called to her. "I'm in the living room."

She walked into the room. "Hello, Jim. How was the drive?"

"Frustrating."

She took off her coat and sat down across from Jim. "Want to explain?"

"Not now. I just came from Ted's office and am declaring a moratorium on the Winters case until after dinner, when I will annoy the hell out of you with my endless speculating."

"Can't wait." She rose. "I have to pee."

"Take your time. I'm not going anywhere."

Jim spared Pat some of the details of his visit with Melanie Johnson, leaving out the part about the kebabs. "On the surface, she seems open, but she keeps most of herself well-hidden."

"Most people do, Jim."

"Not true. Some people inflict their personalities on others because they can't stand themselves."

"More cynical than usual, are we?"

"No, as cynical as usual. You usually don't notice my cynicism because I do such a good job of hiding it."

Pat let out a guffaw.

They stayed at Jim's that night, going to bed early because Jim was tired from the drive and because he had to get up early to meet Sasha Cohen at The Long Gone.

"Sasha adores you," Pat said to Jim when he told her.

"Nonsense."

"All young women adore you, Jim. I'll bet Melanie Johnson misses you at this very moment."

"You're out of your mind."

"And I would be jealous of Sasha if you two were closer in age."

"Are you saying younger women are off-limits to me?"

"All women are off-limits to you. They have to get past me, and that will never happen. Goodnight, Jim."

*

Sasha looked harried when she walked in The Long Gone next morning.

"This has to be quick, Jim. Turmoil in the newsroom."

"Good to see you, too."

"You know what I mean."

"I do, and you'll thank me later. I have a Pulitzer Prize-caliber idea for you."

She raised an eyebrow. "Oh?"

"**The Tobin Bridge Kidnapper and His Disappearing Victim.** One longish piece. What do you think?"

"What would you get out of it?"

"If it's done right, the story might unearth characters who haven't been discovered yet, like Micky Owens's daughter, Abigail."

"He had a daughter? You know this for a fact?"

"Micky's sister told me."

"He had a sister?"

"Who lives on a Native American reservation."

"A dead kidnapper, his missing victim, and a sister who lives on a Native American reservation. Now you're talking. Tell me everything you know."

For the next twenty minutes, as The Long Gone filled up with coffee-to-goers and early morning lap-toppers, he told Sasha what he had discovered.

"Jim," she said, when he paused for breath, "I really have to go, but I'm interested. Let me mull over story angles and get back to you." She stood. "You have been keeping busy. Good for you."

"I could do your job."

"Better than I could, probably."

"Except that I lack your writing skills."

She smiled. "Modesty? From the feared Judge Randall?"

"Rely on your gavel, not your intelligence, was my motto on the bench."

Jim didn't hear anything from Sasha for two weeks. When she called, he was walking on Beauty Shop Row wondering whether he should get an eyebrow weave or a waxing.

"Guess what? My editor liked your idea so much she assigned it to what we are calling our Flashlight Team, a new mini-team of investigative reporters."

"No kidding?"

"She said the story has nooks and crannies galore and a mystery hook. You *could* do my job."

"Don't be silly. I was joking."

"So am I. Our Spotlight Team won a Pulitzer for its investigative work, so any story by a spawn of the team is likely to get wide play, but the Flashlight Team is new and feeling its way. Be patient."

"Thank you, Sasha. One thing I ask: before the story appears change the identifying characteristics of the sister. She has gone to great lengths to remove herself from the world she grew up in, and I don't want to violate her privacy. This is important to me."

"Okay, Jim. I'll see to it."

Jim was not good at killing time. He had trained himself to be patient when a judge, but being patient hadn't come naturally to him. Especially at the beginning of his judgeship, he frequently cut off a long-winded attorney's questioning, eventually learning that good trial lawyers know how to lull a witness into complacency before springing the trap. Of course there were times when the best way to get at the truth was to hammer, hammer, hammer, question after question, showing no mercy, until the resolve of the witness wilted; it depended on the witness and the circumstances of the case. The best attorneys knew when to lay low, when to use a stiletto, and when to use a hammer.

The seasoned Judge Randall had known how to pace a trial. He was in his third-floor study, thinking of this and other things, when Ted Conover called.

"How's your weekend so far?" Ted began.

"Other than feeling washed up and useless, I'm doing fine."

"I called to tell you a young man's badly decomposed body was found wedged in the rocks between Middle Brewster and Outer Brewster Islands. We haven't been able to determine the young man's identity yet, but he was approximately the same age as Aaron Winters. I thought you would want to know as soon as possible, so I am interrupting your undoubtably idyllic weekend to tell you."

"How easy will it be to identify the deceased's identity?"

"Difficult, I'm afraid. Between water immersion and being food for fishes, the fingerprints are gone. We are working the DNA now to see if it's in our data base."

"Are you going to need Edgar Winters's DNA?"

"I hope not. I don't think he would volunteer a sample. You know him better than I do. What do you think?"

"He'll explode. Do your job, stop bothering me, he'll say, but I'm willing to try."

"I don't believe in human sacrifices, but if we need his DNA, I'll let you know."

Jim went downstairs where Pat was reading the Sunday papers at the kitchen table.

"A young man's body has been found in Boston Harbor."

"That's interesting."

"Interesting? That's all you can say?"

"I won't get my hopes up."

"I want to take a drive this afternoon. I'm in an historical mood. Want to come?"

"Where to?"

"The Fruitlands Museum."

"This has to do with the case, doesn't it?"

"Maybe."

"You don't fool me."

"I never try."

The environs of Boston were still lush and green when Pat and Jim drove west. They skirted Concord and West Concord, inched around the busy rotary at the Concord Correctional Facility, then increased speed on the open road past the rotary.

"What I want to do is get into the mind of Mickey Owens's sister, Mavis."

"Be prepared to fail, Jim. Your track record as an amateur sleuth is impressive, but this case was not made for you."

"Whose idea was it to go on this drive?"

"Yours."

"Great idea. Gives us together time."

"Which I treasure. I've been thinking, I'll bet that Aaron Winters died during the kidnapping. Maybe he tried to escape and Micky Owens shot him. That could explain why we haven't heard from him, and why Owens took his own life. The odds are slim that the body found in Boston Harbor is Aaron's."

"You're always so practical."

"One of us has to be."

Fruitlands was a sprawling complex on a hilly piece of land, featuring exhibits devoted to the Shakers, Transcendentalists, and Native Americans. Jim wanted to see the Native American collection again because of his phone call with Mavis Owens. What had Mavis told him? That her bother Micky had a daughter named Abigail. She didn't know Abigail's last name or where she lived.

Standing in the Native American exhibit, Jim tried to absorb the spirit of the Native American world. The line between the real world and the spirit world seemed less distinct in Native American thought than in Jim's world, where reasoning from facts and law reigned supreme.

Could Micky Owens have entrusted his motherless daughter, Abigail, to his sister, Mavis, to raise? Jim could imagine a man like Owens, who was in and out of prison, wanting nothing to do with raising a child, and thinking it was better entrust his daughter to a sister in the Spirit Creek Nation than to a foster family in Massachusetts.

He became aware of Pat standing beside him. "Sorry, I'm trying to imagine a child named Abigail being raised by Mavis Owens in the Spirit Creek Nation."

"Jim, I'm used to you. No apologies necessary."

"I don't think the chronology supports that theory. If I remember correctly, Abigail was born before Mavis joined the Spirit Creek Nation."

"But Mavis could have been raising Abigail already and taken her along when she joined the Nation."

"I think she would have told me if that were the case. That's big. Okay, I've seen enough of the exhibit. Let's head home."

When they were in Jim's car going east on Route 2, Pat said, "To play devil's advocate, why would Mavis accept the responsibility of raising a child? From what you told me, she is someone who totally renounced the world she grew up in, who wouldn't want a living reminder of that world in her life."

"I'm grasping at straws. Don't keep shooting me down."

Jim's phone pinged. He lifted the phone from his pocket and handed it to Pat. "Read the text for me, please."

She read. "It's from Ted. They need Edgar Winters's DNA."

*

"You want my DNA?" Edgar Winters phone voice soared with incredulity.

"Yes. To identity a body which might be Aaron's."

"I am getting damn tired of you and your bumbling friends, Judge Randall. My son is dead and nothing will bring him back, as your meddling keeps reminding me. Leave me alone."

"What makes you so sure he's dead?"

"Because I'm a realist. To go this amount of time without hearing from him or whoever took him means he's dead. Goodbye, Judge. No more contact. Do you understand?"

"That went well," Jim said to Pat when the call ended.

"What now?"

"Rummage through his garbage?"

"You must be kidding."

"Of course I am."

They were in Jim's living room, where they had been sitting since returning from Fruitlands.

"Something will come to me. The Great and Wondrous Judge Randall is not at a loss for what to do next, he's just taking a breather."

His phone chimed. Thinking it was Edgar Winters, Jim answered without looking to see who was calling, a rarity for him. It turned out to be Sasha Cohen, asking to meet. "I have an update on your story idea." They arranged to meet at The Long Gone the next morning.

*

Rarely, in Jim's experience, did light stay the same from one moment to the next, except in The Long Gone. Daylight that made it through the dusty windows always seemed tired from the effort, and the interior lighting gave light a bad name. Jim took the dim lighting to say, we are serious people here, hard at work on our laptops, not to be disturbed.

Sasha was backlit by the sun when she walked through the door. The sudden light hurt Jim's eyes.

"Hi." She approached his table. "What's wrong? Why are you squinting?"

"The sun." He gestured towards the door.

She looked to see what he was referring to. Given that the door was now closed, she couldn't tell.

She plunked down across from him. "The Aaron Winters story line that you suggested is coming along nicely. The young pups on my team are so eager these days, I couldn't hold them back even if I wanted to."

"You're not much older than they, Sasha."

"I feel like their grandma."

"Update me."

"The kids did some digging into Micky Owens. Given his lengthy rap sheet there's a lot there, but he was always a cog in a machine, never the boss. Name a petty crime and the chances are he served time for it. You've heard of perpetual students? Micky Owens was a perpetual petty crook, in and out of prison. He was released from prison on compassionate grounds shortly before he kidnapped Aaron Winters because he only had a few months to live. Which proved to be correct, but not because of illness. Cancer didn't kill him, the Tobin Bridge did. Half my team thinks Owens jumped, half say he was pushed. Neither makes entire sense. Either way, the team is sure the kidnapping was not Owens's idea. He was put up to it."

"No surprises so far," Jim said.

"Then the team traced Owens's sister to the Spirit Creek Nation, but at your request, did not seek to question her. She has lived there for two decades and rarely leaves, making it unlikely she had anything to do with the kidnapping. Lastly, they couldn't find any trace of Micky Owens's daughter, Abigail. None, zero. The team looked for birth records but not knowing the location or date of birth, they struck out. They'll keep looking, but don't get your hopes up."

"Disappointing, though not surprising."

"Good news is the story will run next month. Unsolved mysteries are the most popular and this one's got everything – career crook, a brazen kidnapping, a missing student, and a jump from the Tobin Bridge. Who knows? Maybe the story will unearth a secret or two."

8

The leaves hadn't yet turned and the humidity felt more like summer than fall when the two part story ran. The first part recounted the kidnapping and disappearance of Aaron Winters, the death by Tobin Bridge of Micky Owens, and the steps taken so far by law enforcement to find Aaron Winters. The second part sketched the cast of characters, raising more questions than answers. The series was skillfully done, and Jim praised Sasha highly and deservedly (she deferred the praise to the team of young reporters). It drew a lot of attention at first, being picked up by news outlets in other parts of the country. There was fleeting talk of a TV mini-series. The whereabouts of daughter Abigail became a sort of guessing game on social media and led to dozens of tips to law enforcement agencies around the country, none of which panned out. Then, after several news cycles and hyperbole-to-the-max, the maw of the press masticated the last of the morsels, and the story vanished as if it had never appeared.

Jim and Pat sat at the diningroom table in Vermont, reading the local paper. As disappointed as Jim was not to have solved the mystery of Aaron Winters, it was a relief to read hyper-local news of store closings and school budgets.

"Would you believe the store that sells my prepared foods is closing? What am I going to do for dinner when I'm up here alone?"

"Eat out?"

"Always the rationalist. Why has Aaron Winters's disappearance affected me so much? I can't stop wondering where he is, even though I've accepted we may never find him."

"You witnessed his kidnapping, that's why you can't let it go."

"There's truth in that, but it's also because he made a deep impression on me. I had an immediate sense when Aaron walked in The Long Gone that I could help him. From what I could learn from Melanie Johnson, Aaron is a very smart young man who fears his father. I understand why: Edgar Winters can't imagine how anybody – especially a son of his – could fail to be swayed by the logic of numbers, and Aaron resents being intellectually bullied. I'd be a better father for Aaron than his father."

"Jim, you have good values and if you had kids, you would be a great father, but at times your kids would find you distant because you live so much in your own thoughts."

"You would make a good mother."

"No, I wouldn't. You're wrong. I would make a good aunt, but I don't have mothering instincts. I'm too insular."

The phone rang.

"I never get calls up here," Jim said.

"Well? Are you going to answer it?"

He got up from the table and went to the phone. A landline was a necessity in Vermont because the many ridges and valleys made cell phone service problematic. "Hello?"

"Jim, it's Sasha. A woman called claiming to be the daughter of Micky Owens. She gave her name as Abigail.

Since we didn't give the daughter a name in our story, I tend to believe her. Do you want her number?"

"Yes, I do. What was your sense of her?"

"Her voice was tentative, hesitant. She sounded as if she wanted to run and hide, as opposed to the self-promoters we've heard from since the story ran."

"Yes, give me her number. Thanks, Sasha."

Jim got off the phone and went to the long window in the living room. The Connecticut River was barely visible at this hour of day. Never the same river twice, the philosopher Heraclitus had said. So true, retired judge Jim Randall says.

"What did Sasha want?" Pat asked, interrupting Jim's idle musings.

Jim turned from the window. "A woman claiming to be Micky Owens daughter contacted her. Sasha seemed to believe her. I have her number."

"Are you going to call her?"

"I think so. Yes, I am. Yes, I'm going to call her."

"Why wouldn't you?"

"I'm going to."

He went into the bedroom to collect his thoughts. Gentle, he needed to be gentle. If indeed the woman was Micky Owens's daughter, his crimes weren't her fault.

He lifted the bedroom phone. Then and not before, he noticed that Abigail's area code was 802. She had called Sasha from Vermont.

"Hello?" Abigail's voice was as Sasha had said, the voice of a woman who would rather be doing anything other than talking to a stranger on the phone.

"This is Judge Jim Randall. Sasha Cohen of the *Boston Globe* said you called about your father."

"Yes?" A question, not an answer.

"Your father was Micky Owens?"

"Yes." An answer this time.

"I'm sorry for your loss. Did Sasha explain why I want to learn more about him?"

"She said you are trying to find a college student my father is said to have kidnapped before he died."

"That's correct. Edgar Winters and I were classmates in college. He asked for my help with his son, Aaron, which is why I was in the coffee shop with Aaron when your father took him."

"You were there? You saw it happen?"

"Yes."

"How did my father seem to you?"

"Gruff and unwell."

Abigail's tone of voice changed from present to past. "I hardly knew my father. He left my mother soon after I was born. I only saw him twice that I remember. I know so little about him."

"I'd like to meet you. I notice you have a Vermont area code. Where are you?"

"Rutland."

"That's not far from me. Can we meet?"

"I'm not sure. The reason I didn't contact the police when I read about the kidnapping and my father's death was because I didn't want to get entangled in the life of a man I barely knew, especially a man who was an habitual criminal."

"But you called Sasha Cohen, so you must have changed your mind."

Hesitantly, "Do you know where the Rutland public library is?"

"No, but I can find it." Jim tried to lighten the mood. "Can we talk above a whisper?"

He thought he detected a smile. "I'm the head librarian. We can talk in my office."

*

Abigail, in person, had short brown hair and vigilant eyes behind rimless glasses. Jim liked authentic, but Abigail struck him as almost too authentic for her own good. She looked older than she sounded on the phone.

She extended her hand. "My office is in back. How was your drive?"

"Easy. My house is just north of Brattleboro."

She glanced at him. "You don't look like a hippie."

Brattleboro is a throwback to the sixties, where hippies go who can't shed their hippie ways. Jim had never been a hippie and certainly was not one now but he flashed Abigail a peace sign. Which made her smile. Her smile made Mona Lisa's enigmatic smile seem over-the-top.

She led him into her office, which was behind the fiction shelves. The office was tiny but Abigail had made space for a little round table and two chairs, and that's where she and Jim sat.

"I don't know your last name," Jim said.

That almost-smile again. "Ryan."

"Abigail Ryan suits you."

"Which is lucky because that's my name. I took my mother's last name. Tell me about yourself."

"I was a judge on the Superior Court of Massachusetts for twenty-one years. I live primarily in Cambridge, Massachusetts. I have a significant other who also was a judge on the court, Pat Knowles. You'd like her. What else do you want to know?"

"How did you get into the detective business?"

"Keep in mind that I'm an amateur detective, and a self-appointed one at that."

"How did you get into the self-appointed amateur detective business?"

Jim was changing his mind about her. She had a sense of humor, well-buried but real. Lesson learned: never judge a librarian by her cover.

"Like most big events in a person's life, I fell into sleuthing by accident. I defended a young man in court after I retired as a judge, and one thing led to another." Jim shifted his weight in the chair. "But I came here to ask about you. May I begin?"

"Please. Gently."

"What do you remember about your father?"

"Primarily what my mother told me, and she told me very little. She made him sound like a lost soul who couldn't accept love. There was anger in her voice when she spoke about him, but underneath the anger was regret."

"Where was he at the time?"

"She didn't know. She doubted that he stayed in one place for very long. I think she regretted ever getting involved with him. It was a very brief fling, she told me;

a one-night stand, I later came to realize. She loved me, I never doubted that, but I'm quite sure that if she had it to do over again, she wouldn't have gotten pregnant and especially not by a man she barely knew."

"You speak of your mother in the past tense. Is she alive?"

"No. She died was I was sixteen. That was the first time I met my father. He came to her funeral. I don't know how he learned of it. At first, I didn't know who he was, but little by little it dawned on me, and he confirmed his identity. I didn't feel comfortable talking to him. He seemed dodgy, always looking over his shoulder. I sensed fear and flight."

"You said you saw him twice. When was the second time?"

"Judge Randall, I haven't told anyone what I'm about to tell you, and you must promise to keep it to yourself, okay? Dad came to see me just before the kidnapping. How he found me, I don't know. He looked awful, just terrible. He said he had been released from prison because he had terminal cancer and wanted to make amends before it was too late. The biggest regret in his life was not being a father to me while I was growing up, he said. He hoped I would forgive him."

"What did you tell him?"

"I told him I needed to know him better to forgive him. He said there was no time for that. He teared up when he said that, I almost felt sorry for him, but I couldn't forget that he had abandoned us. I had buried my feelings about not having a father for so long that it was hard to feel anything for him, but with him there in front of me, I felt pity. Pity and sorrow, for the waste of a life. But no anger. Anger seemed beside the point."

"Why didn't you go to the police when you learned of his death?"

"As I told you over the phone. I didn't want to get entangled in the crimes of a man I barely knew. And by then, I was angry. Why wait until he was just about to die before contacting me? Why?"

"Shame, perhaps? He had not led a proud life. I'm curious, given your reluctance to acknowledge him, why are you telling me now?"

"Because Sasha Cohen said you would understand, and because you are gruff."

Jim didn't fully agree – gruff on the surface, maybe – but he wasn't about to argue with her. "Anything else you can tell me about your father?"

"Before he left he said whatever I heard about him in the future, remember that he did it for me."

"What did you make of that? Did he explain what he meant?"

"No, he didn't. He wanted to make amends as best he could, that's all he said. I had no idea what he was about to do."

"Do you understand why he did it?"

"Yes, I think so. After he died I received a certified check in the mail for $3,000, made out to him and endorsed by him to me. I didn't cash the check, because I had no idea who paid him that much money or what it represented. So I held onto it."

"Do you still have it?"

"Yes, it's in my safety deposit box."

"This is important. I would like to tell the DA what you told me. May I?"

"I ask you not to, at least for now. What I hope you will do is use what I have told you to find Aaron Winters. I would like to know if he is still alive. My father was a weak man who did many bad things, but I hope and pray he was not a killer. Once you find Aaron alive, you are free to tell the DA."

"May I tell Sasha Cohen, the journalist behind the series that led you to contact me?"

"If you trust her to keep my secret."

"I do. May I discuss this with Pat, my partner?"

"Of course."

Jim left the library with one question answered and another raised. He felt certain that Micky Owens had kidnapped Aaron Winters for the $3,000, but who paid Owens? Given the marginal life Owens led, $3,000 must have seemed a considerable amount, an amount that might make his estranged daughter think more kindly of him if he left it for her when he died.

He arrived at his house on the hillside before sunset. What was he going to do for dinner given the closure of the grocery store that sold prepared foods? Eat out, Pat had told him. But he didn't want to eat out, he wanted to eat at his table, with a bottle of Cotes du Rhone open before him and the Connecticut River Valley fading to black out the window.

He called Pat. "My meeting with Abigail went well. Very interesting. I'll tell you about it after I eat, but there's nothing in the refrigerator."

"Eat out."

"That's what you said earlier. But I don't want to eat out, I want to eat right here."

"Jim, I'm sure you'll figure something out."

"I will, but I want pampering, and you're not obliging."

"There's nothing at all in the fridge?"

"I think there are some eggs."

"There's your dinner. You know how to make scrambled eggs."

"Yes, I do. I make excellent scrambled eggs.."

"Enjoy your excellent scrambled eggs and call me afterwards. Tell me how your dinner went."

"And my talk with Abigail."

"Yes, tell me that too."

9

After his compassionate release from prison until his fateful encounter with Tobin Bridge, Micky Owens had lived in a boarding house in Somerville, a cash-in-advance kind of place where anonymity was prized more highly than conviviality. The police had questioned the boarders and staff of the rooming house, hoping without success to get a clue where Micky Owens had taken Aaron Winters.

Jim had no reason to duplicate their efforts, but he wanted to get a sense of Micky Owens's world after he got out of prison, so on Jim's return from Vermont he took an unfamiliar bus route to an unfamiliar part of Somerville that lay in the shadow of an elevated highway within sight of abandoned factory buildings. More Charles Sheeler than Norman Rockwell.

Whoever owned the boarding house was apparently bound by a do-not-resuscitate-the- building order which precluded even cosmetic improvements like paint. Standing beneath the elevated highway, feeling the unceasing rumble and roar of traffic above his head, staring at the rooming house where Micky Owens had lived in the weeks between his release from prison and his death, Jim understood the allure of a leap from Tobin Bridge.

Had Edgar Winters visited Micky Owens in prison? Had Winters dangled $3,000 in front of Owens? A haughty, brainy academic visiting Concord State Prison and hiring a small-time crook to kidnap his son? Hard to imagine, but

Edgar was so sure of himself that he might have risked it. But why? It made no sense in the world of everyday reality, but in the 'what you see ain't what you get' world of quantum mechanics – where a particle can simultaneously be here and there – it might make perfect sense.

Time to rattle Professor Winters's cage again.

Winters wasn't happy to see him. "Haven't you bothered me enough?"

"Not quite. How have you been?"

Winters swiveled his office chair to face Jim. "What do you want this time?"

"I'm going on the assumption that your son is still alive, but to prove that, I need your help."

"We've been through this before."

"And since then, you've had time to reconsider and will do all you can to help me, I'm sure. Isn't that right?"

Winters grew indignant. "Do you realize how busy I am? Do you have a clue? I am putting the finishing touches on two papers for scientific journals, writing the keynote address for the annual meeting of the Quantum Society, preparing lectures for an advanced course I'm going to teach next semester, and teaching two classes a week. And you expect me to give thought to my ungrateful son?"

"I'm glad to see you have your priorities straight."

Winters was apparently unfamiliar with irony. "Thank you. Maybe I had you wrong."

Jim internally rolled his eyes. "I take it you haven't heard from Aaron."

"Correct, I haven't. You are working on the assumption he's alive, my assumption is that he's dead. I grieve, then move on."

"My understanding of quantum mechanics is minuscule, but is it possible your son is simultaneously alive and dead?"

"Is that supposed to be funny?"

"Yes, but this isn't. Somebody paid $3,000 to have your son kidnapped. Was it you?"

"$3,000? What are you talking about?"

"That was Micky Owens's fee for kidnapping your son."

"How do you know that?"

"None of your business."

"You're talking about my son, it is my business."

"Apparently I am paying more attention to your son than you are. Oh, I forgot, you think he's dead. So sad, but you're too busy to mourn. Good day, Professor. I will keep looking for your son. If you change your mind and want to help, you know how to contact me."

It was a relief for Jim to find himself outside building E73 even though that part of campus bore a resemblance to where Micky Owens had roomed, minus the elevated highway. Had he rattled Winters? Hard to tell.

Next, Sasha Cohen. Sasha couldn't see him until late afternoon. They met at The Long Gone. *She* looked rattled.

"What's wrong, Sasha?"

"Yesterday I learned that I'm pregnant."

"Congratulations! That's wonderful. You and your husband must be very excited."

"He is. I'm scared. What if something goes wrong?"

"I assume you've had all the tests?"

"And all looks good, but what if there are complications?" She looked as if she were about to cry.

"Everything will be fine, you shouldn't worry."

"What if something is wrong that doesn't show up on the tests?"

"Sasha, you are one of the strongest people I know. You and your husband will get through whatever happens, but I've got a feeling you'll give birth to a happy, healthy child. I'm predicting a girl."

She smiled a little. "I like the sound of that. Okay, tell me about your meeting with Micky Owens's daughter."

"I think it went well." Jim told her most if not all of what Abigail had told him. Sasha scribbled notes as Jim talked. When he finished, she looked up from her notes. "I take it Abigail has no idea where Aaron Winters is?"

"None. My gut tells me Aaron's still alive. Maybe I'm wrong, but I see Micky Owens as a dying ex-con who only became a kidnapper to leave $3,000 to his daughter. I don't see him as a killer."

"I assume your next move is to learn who paid Micky Owens the $3,000?"

"Correct."

"What's your guess?"

"Aaron's father."

"To what purpose?" Sasha asked.

"To scare Aaron into following his advice and staying at MIT? To punish Aaron for disobeying his advice? To take credit for obtaining his son's release from his kidnapper? I don't know, I'm grasping at straws, but Edgar Winters is not recognizably human. He is a walking, talking algorithm, who can't be understood in human terms. I see him as capable of doing anything that will help him get what he wants."

"Jim, I have to go to work. Pregnant or not, I've still got a job to do. Thanks for talking me off the expectant mother cliff, and don't lose your objectivity. Okay?"

"I hear you."

"Really? Do you?"

"Yes, Sasha, I do."

They parted outside The Long Gone. He watched her go, glad their paths had crossed early in his career as an amateur sleuth.

Pat had a neighborhood meeting to attend that night. Her Beacon Hill neighbors were up in arms about something; they were always up in arms about something: street lighting, crosswalks, signage; the smaller the stakes, the greater the outrage. Cambridge residents were even worse. Intellect was no guarantee of good judgement.

He ate at the bar at Duck, Duck, Goose. "I'm alone tonight, Bruce. Pat's abandoned me for the night."

"How dare she? Table or bar?"

"I haven't eaten at the bar for a while. Bar."

"You got it."

The horseshoe-shaped bar at Duck, Duck, Goose had eight stools, an eating-alone or pre-dinner-drink bar, not a settle-in-and-get-drunk bar. Chris the bartender/ sommelier prided himself on recommending wines to his regulars.

"Haven't seen you for a while, Judge. I was hoping to get your opinion on a 2015 Cahors from a family winery in the southwest of France."

"Be glad to try it."

"Sorry, I decided not to carry it. Eating with us tonight?"

"Yes, please."

Chris pulled a menu from under the counter and handed it to Jim. "No specials tonight."

Jim had been eating more red meat than was good for him, so he ordered chicken. Something had nagged him since his meeting with Abigail. Even if he could nudge it into his consciousness, could he trust what Abigail had told him? In a courtroom there were exhibits and cross-examinations, tried-and-true ways to test a witness' credibility; in detective work there weren't. It was seat-of-your-pants work, liberating in a way, maddening in another. What was he missing? He was sure it would be obvious once discovered.

The chicken was surprisingly good. He told Chris so before he left.

"Thanks, Judge. Don't stay away so long this time."

He walked home slowly, savoring the night. His townhouse was just around the corner, not far at all, but on mellow nights like this, he took his time, stretching out the walk to the max. He didn't have a bad life, which he could forget when he was stuck in the middle of a case. He wondered how Pat's neighborhood meeting was going. Genteel? Screaming? He missed her.

*

Jim took the #69 bus to Ted Conover's office Monday morning. The #69 bus only came every twenty minutes or so, but it had the advantages of a stop on his corner and a drive past Beauty Shop Row and the live poultry store. He got a kick that one could buy a freshly killed chicken and get a facial or a mani-pedi in the mile and a half between Harvard and MIT.

"Dammit, Ted, change something in your office. Don't you have a new family photo you could put on your desk, a new painting of a sailboat you could put on the wall?"

Ted, younger than Jim by a little and handsome in a way that appealed to both men and women without threatening either, turned the question back on Jim. "You can ask me that? You, the most stubborn, inflexible man I have ever known?"

"Not so, I am flexibility incarnate."

Ted turned his head to look at the painting on the wall. "Anyway, the sailboat is sailing against the wind. Symbolism, you old fart."

"Do you want to hear my news or do you want to call me the names you couldn't when I was on the bench?"

"You drive a hard bargain, you old fart."

"I met Micky Owens's daughter, that's my news."

Suddenly, Ted was all business. "You found her? No kidding?"

"No kidding. I met with her. Which is more than your crack team of investigators did."

"What did she tell you?"

"She barely knew her father and doesn't want to get entangled in his legacy. He left mother and daughter very early in the daughter's life, and she only saw him twice after that."

"Does she know anything about the kidnapping?"

"Only what's in the news. She says her father was close to death the last time she saw him. He apologized for not being more of a father to her."

"When was that?"

"Shortly before the kidnapping."

"All very interesting, but how does this help me?"

"It confirms that Micky Owens knew he was dying and had nothing to lose when he kidnapped Aaron Winters. It lends weight to the idea that he didn't hatch the idea of kidnapping Aaron on his own, that somebody hired him."

Ted weighed his words. "Nice work, old friend."

"No longer old fart?"

"Not for the moment."

*

At breakfast next morning, the sunlight through Jim's kitchen windows was so strong it seemed a solid. Jim slid the Metro section of the *Globe* to Pat.

"Look at this." He pointed to the headline on the next-to-the-last page.

HUMAN SKELETON FOUND IN
ABANDONED VERMONT QUARRY

"Aaron Winters perhaps?" Pat said after reading the brief story.

"That's what I'm wondering." He pulled his phone out of his pocket.

"Who are you calling?" Pat asked. "Don't forget it's early."

"I'm not calling anybody. I'm checking the *Rutland Herald* to see how they're covering the story."

The *Rutland Herald* covered the story in detail. The partial skeleton was of a young male, average height, age 20-25. The bones had been discovered hidden under debris in an abandoned slate quarry on the Vermont-New York border. Parts of the skeleton were missing, including the skull.

"I know that area," Jim said, reading his phone.

"What area?" Pat said.

"On the border between New York and Vermont north of Bennington." Jim entered a number on his phone. He put it to his ear. "Now I am calling someone."

"Who?"

"Ted." He shifted the phone to his left ear. "Ted? Jim Randall. Sorry to bother you at such an early hour.... You're right, I'm not sorry, but did you see the story about the buried bones?"

Jim listened for a minute, then clicked off. "Yes, he has seen the story, no, he doesn't know more about it. He's on the way to his office and will let me know if he learns anything."

"Where are you going?" Pat asked when Jim stood up.

"The Long Gone."

The Long Gone was hopping that morning. Not hopping exactly, more like loudly humming. So forget about motion. The Long Gone was loudly humming that morning. Jim took his coffee to a rear table, not the absolute rear, towards the rear. Nothing was as it first seemed that morning.

He opened the *Globe* to its full width; he liked being the only person in The Long Gone reading a print newspaper. See how much news I can scan moving only my eyes, you heathens? No buttons, no clicks, no scrolling, just eyes and brain.

He hoped the bones were not Aaron Winters's. He wanted Aaron to be alive. Jim didn't think his disappearance was a kidnapping gone wrong, there was more to it – the something he had on the tip of his brain just waiting for a nudge. He needed Aaron Winters to be alive so he could solve the kidnapping. You are not a nice man, Jim Randall: you hope Aaron Winters is still alive so you can solve a puzzle, not because you don't want a promising young man to lose his life.

He refolded the paper back to the front page, and laid it on the table beside his coffee.

A moment later, a young man hovered over the space beside Jim. "Excuse me, this is the only vacant space. Do you mind?"

Jim grumbled but moved his paper out of the way.

"Thanks." The young man sat down. Jim got up to go. The young man frowned, prompting Jim to snap at him, "Don't flatter yourself, I'm not leaving because of you."

Jim had misread him. The expression that came over the young man's face was pure chagrin.

Outside The Long Gone, Jim chastised himself. You are losing it, Randall. The young man didn't deserve your wrath. You are angry at yourself for not solving the puzzle. Pull yourself together.

He headed home. Beauty Shop Row would cheer him up, but he didn't feel like taking the long route.

The leaves on his street were losing their green but weren't yet brown. Fade to brown, the stage directions read. He fumbled for his house key.

10

The bones were still unidentified a week later. Aaron Winters was a possible match, but the match was inconclusive. DNA was needed.

"I need your help," Ted said over the phone. "Edgar Winters adamantly refuses to provide us with a sample of his DNA."

"You want me to talk to him, I presume?" Jim said.

"Would you?"

"Yes, but he won't listen. He's dug in. Doesn't trust you guys, is tired of me."

"I don't understand him, Jim. His son is missing, yet he won't help."

"I don't fully get it either. It has something to do with his thinking that if law enforcement knew what it was doing, his son would have been found by now. Competence is everything to this guy."

"Or maybe he doesn't want us to find his son."

"That too."

Jim gave himself a pep talk as he walked to building E73 – don't give Winters a chance to say no, crowd him. He was just getting back from the lecture hall where he taught the popular course, Introduction to Quantum Mechanics – To Be Or Not To Be; The Answer Is Yes.

Winters wasn't looking where he was going when he bumped into Jim. "Sorry," he said, then retracted it when he saw who it was.

"A minute of your time."

They were in the hallway outside Winters's office.

"Not even thirty seconds. I know what you want, and the answer is still no. Now step aside."

Jim followed him into his office. "Don't you want to know if the bones are your son?"

"They are not."

"How can you be sure?"

"The skull is missing, is it not?"

"Yes."

"That sounds ritualistic or sadistic to me. Aaron's kidnapper was a small-time crook who needed a paycheck."

"You sound very sure it's not your son."

"I am sure."

"A DNA test could eliminate doubt."

"No."

"Professor Winters, your refusal won't look good if it hits the *Globe*."

"You wouldn't dare."

Jim gestured to an imaginary headline. "What is the eminent professor afraid of? Does he have something to hide?"

"Get out."

"Think it over, Professor, while there's still time."

*

Slate Valley is a 24 mile long, 6 mile wide valley on the Vermont-New York border, at one time the biggest supplier of colored slate in the world, still the home of 25 companies that mine quarries in the valley. Mountains of rock and debris ring the quarries after the useable slate is mined. In one of those abandoned quarries, the still-unidentified bones had been found.

The *Granville Sentinel* made the story the centerpiece of their paper for the next several editions. Not many mysteries of this magnitude fell into their laps. The piles of debris surrounding abandoned quarries became a subject of fascination for locals and visitors alike. The Slate Valley Museum mounted a temporary exhibit on objects found in quarries through the years.

"I need to see this for myself. Want to come?" Jim asked Pat.

"I'll pass. You'll be preoccupied."

The first half of the drive was on the roads he took to get to his Vermont house. From there he drove over the Green Mountains to Manchester, home of outlet stores like Brooks Brothers and Armani, then on to Slate Valley. The contrasts along the way couldn't be greater.

He stopped for lunch at a diner in Granville, NY. He sat on a stool at the counter, ordered a hot turkey sandwich, and opened *The New York Times* to read while he waited.

The man sitting next to him looked to be in his fifties, thick bodied, soft-spoken. He struck up a conversation.

"Lot of folks around here will think you're a communist, seeing you reading that paper."

Jim stopped reading. "The *New York Times*?"

The man smiled. "Don't worry, I'm non-violent. Where are you from?"

"Cambridge."

"New York?"

"Massachusetts."

"That explains it. The People's Republic of Cambridge."

"Don't believe everything you hear," Jim replied. "Let me ask you a question. What's the scuttlebutt about the bones found in the quarry?"

"Puts this region on the map after decades of being ignored."

"Any theories about the bones? Whose are they, why did they end up here?"

"The prevailing theory is that they were brought here by some flatlander who didn't want them to be found. Who would look for them in an overlooked area like ours? You have a special interest in bones? Are you an anthropologist?"

"Not even close. An ex-judge."

"No kidding. What's being a judge like?"

"The best part was the gavel."

The man's chuckle sounded like the grinding of gears in an old truck. He leaned closer. "Sentence anybody to death?"

"Massachusetts doesn't have the death penalty. Help me out, how do I get to the office of the *Sentinel* from here?"

"Did you come on Route 149?"

"Yes."

"Then you drove right past it. When you leave here, head back the way you came. The *Sentinel* is half-a-mile on the right, at the curve."

The *Sentinel* was in a two-story building that was easy to miss. Jim parked on the street and went in. He told the woman at the first desk who he was and why he was there.

"Richard Mullins is who you want to talk to. He's out at the moment on a story, should be back soon." She reached for her phone. "I'll see if I can reach him."

While Jim waited, he checked his messages. One from Ted.

> Checking out a report from the Indiana
> State Police of a young man matching
> Aaron Winters's description spotted
> at a shopping mall in Terre Haute

"Judge?" The receptionist was speaking to him.

"Yes, sorry." Jim put his phone away.

"Richard's on his way back to the office. He asks you to wait for him."

"Good. Thanks."

"You can sit over there." She pointed to three chairs by the door. "He should be back any minute."

Ten minutes later, a middle-aged man swept through the door. Shorter than Jim, slighter in build, he made up in energy what he lacked in size. He shook Jim's hand. "Richard Mullins."

"Jim Randall. I take it you know why I'm here."

"I do. Your legend precedes you. Do you want to see the quarry in question?"

"Please."

Mullins drove east out of town, turning left onto a dirt road by a gas station. The road led past several house-high piles of discarded slate and loose stone. Mullins parked beside an especially big pile.

"Come on," he said. "Follow me."

The mound was too high and the debris too loose for Jim to safely climb, but Mulligan led him into the abandoned quarry via a narrow path through the rubble. A pool of water filled the bottom of the pit.

"The young man's bones were found here. Two lovers had made their way here and spotted a human-sized pelvis and femur floating in the water. Freaked them out, I was told."

"Had there been any missing person reports here?"

"Not recently, not around here. The prevailing theory is that the murder took place elsewhere and the body dumped where no one would think to look. This mine has been abandoned for years, and you saw for yourself how poor the access is. My guess is the killer is a hunter, used to cutting up carcasses. I think the deceased's head was removed to hide the fact that he had been shot in the head. You want to know my opinion as a journalist who has covered a story or two? These are not the bones of Aaron Winters. Aaron Winters is alive and hiding in plain sight. That's my opinion."

"Interesting," Jim said.

"Want to explore here some more?"

"Just a little. I won't be long."

"Take your time. I'll wait for you in my car."

The pit was surrounded by dense underbrush and thick woods, making it hard for Jim to circle the pit to gain perspective. Jim could not see ten feet ahead of him.

He fought his way back to Richard Mullens's car and climbed in.

"Learn anything?" Mullens asked.

"That I wouldn't make a good deer."

Mullens didn't hide his smile. "You'd better check for ticks when you get wherever you're going."

Mullens dropped Jim off at the *Sentinel* office. Jim climbed out. "Thanks for the help. Here's my card. I'd appreciate a call if you learn anything new."

"Will do, and vice-versa. I'd love to scoop the competition."

Jim only got as far as Manchester before he decided to stop for the night. He'd much prefer to sleep in his own bed, but Brattleboro was over an hour away and he was not a young man. He stayed at a bed and breakfast and ate dinner at a steakhouse, which he knew he shouldn't but did anyway. They only had domestic wine, to his chagrin, but the steak was good.

His room at the bed and breakfast had a small TV, but he didn't turn it on. He preferred to lie on his back with his hands beneath his head, searching for the missing clue that would lead him to Aaron Winters. Only problem was, he didn't have a clue. When his arms beneath his head began to ache, he gave up and turned on the TV. Let's face it, Jim, you're a bad sleuth or the answer would have come to you long before now.

Wait a minute. Maybe I've been making this too complicated. Start simple, add complexity only as needed. Worked in the past, why not now?

He sat up, fully alert. He needed to see Abigail Ryan again. He called her when the Rutland Library opened in the morning.

11

The Rutland Public Library felt familiar to him by now, even though he had only been to it once. Abigail was waiting for him in her tiny office.

"Thanks for agreeing to see me on such short notice. Not until last night did it dawn on me what I was overlooking."

"Which is?"

"The $3,000 bank check you received after your father died. I'd like to see it."

Abigail shook her head. "I'm sorry. I'm truly sorry, but I still don't want to be involved."

"You're involved whether you like it or not."

"But you'll tell the police, and I'll be questioned."

"Sooner or later they'll find out. You said you didn't cash the check, that it's in your safety deposit box. If you won't show me, at least tell me what bank it's drawn on."

"You're not going to give up, are you?" She paused, then gave a shrug. "Okay."

"Okay what?"

"Okay, I'll show you the check."

It was more or less a straight shot from the library to the bank, which looked more like a library than a bank. Abigail parked in the lot behind the bank.

The safe deposit boxes were in the basement.

Abigail showed her ID, signed in and was led into the vault. Jim stayed behind.

There were cushioned chairs in the waiting area, but they were badly in need of re-upholstering. Jim sat and waited. It took Abigail forever.

She emerged from the vault with a check and an apology for taking so long. "I had forgotten some of the stuff I have in the box. Fascinating. It's like a time capsule."

"Is that the check?"

"Yes." She handed it to him. The issuing bank was the Upper Valley Bank in Burlington, Vermont.

Jim handed it back to Abigail. "Just what I thought."

"What?"

"I know who sent you the money."

"Who?"

"Melanie Johnson. Abigail, you've been a huge help. Thank you."

Abigail drove them back to her library without saying a word. She seemed subdued, chastened. They parted in the parking lot. "Thanks again," Jim said. Abigail did not linger. When she had gone, Jim stood on the sidewalk, assessing his mistake. Edgar Winters had not paid Mickey Owens to kidnap his son. Jim knew that now. Edgar Winters was a thoroughly obnoxious individual, but he wasn't a criminal. Jim had let his feelings get in the way.

He called Pat. "Hi, what are you doing?"

"Writing volume 2 of my memoir. It's taking forever."

"Slow going, huh?"

"Jim, you're calling for a reason, and it's not my memoir. What is it?"

"I'm going to be away longer than I thought. I'm heading up to Burlington when I get off the phone."

"I like Burlington."

"I do too. Too bad you didn't want to join me on my trip up here."

"I didn't know you would be going to Burlington. How long do you think you'll stay?"

"Depends how cooperative Melanie Johnson is."

"Want to explain?"

"I'll explain when I know I'm right. I've been wrong about this case from the start."

Pat didn't answer.

"Pat? Are you there?"

"You have just defined 'deep end' for me, as in, 'go off the'..."

"All will become clear when Melanie answers a few questions."

On the road from Rutland to Burlington, Lake Champlain came into view north of Middlebury. Jim remembered the expansive waters from the first time he and Pat visited Melanie Johnson.

She would not want to see him again when she learned what he wanted.

So true. "No, no, and no way. This is too painful for me. Aaron and I ended our engagement and now he is missing. What more do you want from me?"

"The truth would be helpful."

The line went dead.

He had called from a parking lot on the Burlington waterfront. The lapping waters of Lake Champlain said: calm down, take a load off. Chill.

He took a room at the first hotel he came to. It was on the waterfront, but his room overlooked the roof of a parking garage.

He stretched his tired frame out on the bed. After a moment, he reached for his phone and texted Melanie.

> Truth-time, Melanie. You know where
> Aaron is. If there are extenuating
> circumstances, I'll take them into
> account, but first you must
> tell me where he is.

He put the phone on his bed and waited. She didn't respond for twenty minutes.

Than his phone dinged with a text from Melanie.

> You have lost your mind.

Jim replied:

> Suit yourself. You can cooperate or you
> can withhold evidence. Either way I'm
> going to the DA.

> You're bluffing. You know nothing.

> I know that Abigail, the kidnapper's daughter,
> received a cashiers check for $3,000 from a
> Burlington bank shortly after the kidnapping.
> I believe that the check was drawn on your
> account. The DA can subpoena the bank and
> quickly determime if I'm right.

A delay so long Jim was about to admit defeat. Then,

Do you remember the coffee shop where we
met the first time?

Yes.

Meet me there in thirty minutes.

The coffee shop was on the pedestrian shopping street high above the lake. Jim got there early and waited outside. Melanie arrived a few minutes later, looking like a harried college student late for a class.

"I'm not happy to see you again," she said, leading the way into the brightly lit coffee shop.

They took a table near the door.

"Why can't you leave well enough alone?" she began.

"I'm too close to the answer."

"What answer? Micky Owens is dead. Aaron is missing. Nothing has changed nor is likely to change in the near future. Why not leave it alone?"

"I believe Aaron is alive, I believe the kidnapping was his idea, and I believe you paid his kidnapper."

Melanie sputtered. "Ridiculous. Rubbish pure and simple."

"The purpose of the kidnapping was to make Aaron's father think he's dead, so he would leave Aaron alone once and for all. One thing I don't understand, how did Aaron find a small time hood like Micky Owens?"

"Let me turn the question around. Why would a small time hood like Micky Owens agree to such a ridiculous scheme?"

"Because Owens was dying and this was his chance to leave money to the daughter he had abandoned at birth. It was his attempt to make amends."

"And supposedly you used to be a judge, devoted to reason. Is that true? Is that possible?" she said..

Jim kept his voice down. "Where has Aaron been hiding? Is he here in Burlington with you?"

Scorn. Shock and scorn. "Don't be ridiculous."

"You have overused the word ridiculous, but you haven't answered my questions."

"Judge, may I remind you that Aaron and I broke up before this all began. We had called off our engagement. We were finished, done. Why would I help him?"

"I don't believe you broke up. I think the breakup was as fake as the kidnapping."

Melanie shook her head. "You are going to feel like such a fool when you find out how wrong you are. I've lost respect for you, Judge." She stood to go. "For the last time, leave us alone."

Jim stayed in his seat, considering her words. Leave us alone, she had said. Us, not me. His phone rang. Jim stepped outside to take the call.

"Jim, it's Ted. Where are you?"

"Burlington, Vermont. Having just met with Melanie Johnson. I now can confirm with confidence that Aaron Winters is alive."

"You might want to reserve judgement on that. Remember the sighting in Terra Haute of a young man who resembles Aaron Winters?"

"Of course."

"The young man was arrested late last night for robbing a convenience store and, get this, the authorities are convinced he is Aaron Winters."

"Does he acknowledge that?"

"No, he swears he's not. His prints are being checked right now. You may have been wrong about this one, Jim."

"I may have been, but I think not. Let's wait and see."

Jim went back inside. His coffee was cold. He took his cup to the counter to get a refill. The young woman at the counter was inordinately cheerful. She almost broke into song. "Isn't it a gorgeous day, sir? Burlington at its best! Enjoy the rest of your day."

"I shall try my best."

Jim left the coffee house without finishing his coffee. He walked downhill towards his hotel, thinking that the young woman at the counter had been right, the day was beautiful. The waning sun rippled off the deep blue waters of Lake Champlain. Hard to be depressed on such a day, but Jim gave it a try. It would be a singular blow to his pride if he were wrong about the son after being wrong about the father.

Jim ate a quick dinner then lay down on his bed to take his mind off the Winters, father and son, by watching crappy television . Fortunately Blue Bloods reruns were on that night, so it wasn't all crappy. He waited until Pat likely had finished dinner before calling. "Where did you eat?" he asked when he reached her.

"My apartment. How about you?"

"At the diner where we ate breakfast when we were in Burlington."

"You ate someplace where they didn't have wine?"

"They have wine, Pat."

"Any good?"

"Lousy. Oh, the missing young man in Terra Haute has been found, and the police think he's Aaron Winters. I don't. I think Aaron is alive and well and hiding with his girlfriend in Burlington."

"Have you seen him?"

"No. But I will."

"I hope you're right. What's your agenda for the evening?"

"Blue Bloods reruns."

"I like Blue Bloods."

"Correction. You like Jamie Reagan. You think he's cute."

"He is cute, Jim. You can't deny that."

"He's not bad, but compared to me, he's ordinary."

"You are majestic, it's true. Goodnight, Jim."

Jim woke up refreshed and went downstairs to the hotel coffee shop for breakfast, feeling more settled in mind than he had since he witnessed Aaron Winters being forced from The Long Gone at gunpoint. Something had happened in Jim's brain while he slept, some assembling of the puzzle pieces allowing him to make sense of Aaron's kidnapping from beginning to now, from The Long Gone in Cambridge, Massachusetts, to a hotel coffee shop in Burlington, Vermont. Breakthroughs justify big breakfasts: scrambled eggs with bacon and home fries, two pancakes, orange juice and coffee. Pat would be appalled, but once in a while, why not? Man does not live by big biscuit shredded wheat alone.

After breakfast he walked the rest of the way down College Street to the waterfront park he had glimpsed from the hotel. The park looked inviting, green and spacious, with benches overlooking Lake Champlain. Just what he needed to plan his final moves. He picked a bench next to a large museum-like building from which people came and went. When he was settled on the bench, he texted Ernie Farrell.

> I need you to do your magic.
> Find out where Melanie Johnson works.
> Some sort of office in Burlington, VT.
> Graduated from MIT last spring.

Jim stretched his arms out on the bench, leaned his head back, and took in the sun. Life was good again. Given that he had been wrong until now, he couldn't imagine why he felt so confident, but he did. Ernie's answer came while Jim's eyes were closed.

> Too easy, give me something harder.
> Melanie Jackson works at ECHO,
> Leahy Center for Lake Champlain,
> 1 College Street on the waterfront.

College Street. That was the street he had walked to get to the waterfront park. Jim wondered if the large, museum-like building across the street from him was the Leahy Center. Jim got off his bench to take a look. A science and nature museum, he saw when he got closer. The address? 1

College Street. The luck of the amateur detective. Should
he enter and ask for Melanie? To what purpose? It would
piss her off even more to think he was stalking her. He
returned to his bench and waited for Melanie to emerge.

His phone pinged. At first he thought he was imagining
it. It pinged again. A text from Ted.

The Terra Haute suspect is not our guy.
Fingerprints don't match.

Jim was glad. He wanted to be the one to solve this case,
to make up for thinking Edgar Winters was the culprit. He
sat on his bench and closed his eyes. Don't doze off, he told
himself.

He became alert when he realized there was activity at
the entrance to the museum. A school group had gathered,
waiting to go in. As Jim watched the kids, Melanie left the
building and walked uphill on College Street. Jim followed
at a discreet distance.

What did he think he was doing? This was carrying an
avocation too far. He was not an undercover cop stalking
a suspect, nor a PI hired by a jealous husband to keep tabs
on a wife. He was an out-of-shape, aging ex-judge who
should know better.

As he watched, Melanie ducked into a drugstore.
Jim waited outside. A few moments later, she reemerged,
carrying a small paper bag the size of a prescription bottle.
She turned back downhill towards the science museum.

He felt like a fool. It was not a crime to fill a prescription.

He watched until Melanie reached her museum. She
stopped at the entrance; the lake sparkled beyond her.

Jim was about to turn away when he saw a young man approach her, a man with the kind of dark hair you run your hand through once in the morning then forget about the rest of the day. A man resembling Aaron Winters. Jim hurried towards the young man and Melanie.

As Jim approached, the man spotted him and darted away. Melanie glanced in Jim's direction, then disappeared into the museum. Only then did Jim realize he didn't have a breath to spare. Old Man Randall here, panting for breath, waiting for a walk light on a Burlington street corner. This had to stop. If he was intent on proving his point that Aaron was alive, so be it, but don't kill himself in the process. He called Pat. "I spotted Aaron Winters."

"Where?"

"The Burlington waterfront."

"Are you sure it was him?"

"Yes."

"Sure enough to report it to the police?"

"No."

"Why are you out of breath?"

"I am not young."

"I could have told you that."

"But I'm brilliant. And sexy and charming."

"You should have stopped at not being young. Did Aaron spot you?"

"Yes. My surveillance skills are lacking."

"Is he likely to show himself again, if he knows you're following him?"

"There you go being rational again. I'll call you when I have decided on my next step. It will be wildly improvisational, I assure you."

He waited in the park until he was sure neither Aaron nor Melanie would appear again, returned to his hotel and asked if his room was available another night. It was. He went to the room and texted Melanie. He tried to keep it as casual as possible.

> Are you and Aaron free
> for dinner tonight?

Her response:

> You've got to be kidding.
> Go away.

Jim:

> Believe me, I want to. How about this?
> I won't tell the DA until you and Aaron have
> a chance to tell me your side of the story.
> You and he will be in less trouble if you
> cooperate, than if you don't.

12

He hadn't gotten a response by dinner time. Jim was hungry. A long day of surveillance will do that to you. Where to eat? He and Pat had eaten at a little French bistro on the pedestrian shopping street when they were in Burlington. He remembered the food as acceptable and the wine quite good. Besides, the bistro would remind him of Pat.

He texted her after he was seated at a table. The bistro was three-quarters full.

> Eating dinner at the French bistro where we
> ate when we were in Burlington.

Her reply:

> No more Aaron sightings?

Jim:

> None. I'll come home tomorrow if no
> progress. It's fun running after a young man
> who is presumed dead, but I am not young,
> and I'm done in. I will report what I saw to Ted
> and call the investigation a wrap.

Jim ordered chicken. He had to ask the waitress to decipher the description of how it was prepared but it sounded good when she did. "That's what I'll have. And a glass of the Luberon."

"Very good," she replied. Thank God she didn't say 'perfect,' which seemed the thing to say in restaurants nowadays.

He turned his attention to the *New York Times.* which he brought with him to read while he ate. He doubted that anybody in Burlington would think him a commie for reading *The Times*. They might think of him as a relic for reading it in print, but a communist? Unlikely.

YOU THINK THINGS ARE BAD NOW? JUST WAIT, screamed every headline.

He looked up when he heard his name. "Judge Randall?"

"Yes?" How does the waitress know my name, Jim wondered.

It wasn't the waitress. It was Melanie Johnson. Aaron Winters was with her.

"May we join you?"

Jim seemed not to hear her at first, then he got to his feet, "By all means." The table was for two, so Aaron pulled up another chair and sat at the corner of the table. Jim quickly compared how Aaron looked in this Burlington bistro to how he looked when Micky Owens had hustled him out of The Long Gone. Then he had looked taken aback, a little angry, but not scared. Now he looked scared.

"Hello, Aaron. Good to see that you're alive," Jim said, as casually as he could muster.

Aaron cleared his throat. "I wasn't going to come but Melanie convinced me you wouldn't quit until I did, and that if I could explain my actions to you, I would stand a better chance with the DA."

"She was right. How did you know I'd be eating here?"

"I've been watching you since you came to Burlington."

The waitress brought Jim's glass of wine. "Would either of you like something to drink?" she asked. Melanie and Aaron shook their heads.

Jim asked, "Do you want something to eat?"

"Not for me," Melanie said.

"I would, I'm starving," Aaron said, then turned sheepish. "Mel, would you mind?"

"Of course not, Aaron."

The waitress turned. "I'll bring you a menu."

When she had gone, Jim asked Aaron how long he had been in Burlington,

"I waited a couple of weeks until I was no longer in the news, then I came up. I've been here since."

"It was your plan all along to join Melanie, wasn't it?"

"Yes. Dad disapproved of our getting married, among other things, but I was determined." Aaron glanced in her direction and smiled. "To everyone up here, I'm Jack Holmes, who moved to Burlington because of the tech opportunities. Burlington has become a magnet for techies, so my story rings true."

The waitress brought Aaron the menu. "Tonight's special is pork loin with prunes and brussels sprouts."

Aaron closely studied the menu. "Do you have anything vegetarian?"

"Are you vegan?"

"No."

"Then yes. I would recommend the vegetable lasagna."

"That's what I'll have." He looked at the waitress with what Jim took to be relief: his hunger was for more than food, it was to be done with hiding.

While Jim gauged Aaron's mood, he tasted his wine. Serviceable if not exciting. "Aaron, I think I know why you did what you did, but I want to hear it from you. Why don't you start at the beginning?"

Jim saw Aaron shift gears, as if he had been preparing for this moment. "I'd rather start at the end."

Jim shrugged. "Suit yourself."

Aaron began slowly but picked up speed as he talked. "Because you have met my father, you surely understand. You do, don't you? I had to make a clean break from him, I could not breathe, I could not plan my life, because in my head all I heard from him was, 'no, no, you don't have what it takes, don't make me look bad, you're a student at the university where I am a revered professor, if you drop out you will dishonor me,' etc, etc, until I couldn't take it anymore. I reminded him of the people who have dropped out of college and done pretty well for themselves – Bill Gates, Mark Zuckerberg – but he would have none of it. Can't you understand my frustration?"

"I can," Jim said, "but I also understand your father's point of view. The men you cite had specific plans which they couldn't pursue until they dropped out of college."

"But he wouldn't have left me alone as long he knew where to find me. Don't you see? Dad only tolerates choices he can conceive making for himself. He has zero empathy. Don't ask him to put himself in another's shoes, he doesn't see any shoes other than his own."

Jim nodded. "I do get the impression his world-view doesn't include many people besides himself."

"The only way I could marry Melanie and live the life I wanted was to cut ties entirely, take an assumed name, and start over."

"Couldn't you just say, Dad, I'm taking time off to sort things out. I'll be back to finish school once I find myself."

Aaron snorted. "Are you kidding me, Judge? Do you not understand how limited Dad's understanding of human beings is? You know what he'd say to 'find myself?' He'd say, why do you need to, you're not lost. You're standing right in front of me."

"Did you think you would never be found?"

"I assumed I eventually would, but I hoped enough time would pass for me to get a head start on a new life. I wanted Dad to think I was dead. No halfway measures."

"It's a crime to file a false report, let alone stage a fake crime."

"But isn't the usual penalty a fine?"

"For a false report, yes, but for faking a kidnapping, you'll probably be indicted. Given your clean record and the circumstances, you might get probation, but you might do time."

"Worth the risk." Aaron's food arrived. He dug in.

Jim gave him time. "The one thing I don't understand is how you found Micky Owens. It's not everyday that one runs across an ex-con with a terminal illness."

"I taught coding at the Middlesex Correctional Institute where Micky was incarcerated. After I got to know him, he confided he was dying. He desperately wanted to do something for his daughter, Abigail, before he died. He felt guilty that she grew up without a father. That gave me the idea of a kidnapping which would serve Micky's purpose and mine. We eventually settled on a price of $3,000, enough to pay off Abigail's student loan. I have no money and I certainly couldn't ask my father, but Melanie said she would loan me the money."

"So you two never ended your engagement?"

"To the contrary, we got married soon after I joined Melanie in Burlington."

"Congratulations, but your honeymoon may be short-lived. I have to tell the DA I found you. I assume you anticipated that."

Aaron nodded. "I'm prepared to turn myself in. I knew there was a risk to what I did, but I was willing to take the risk to marry Melanie and start a new life."

"We'll drive to Cambridge tomorrow. Do you promise not to disappear overnight?"

"You have my word."

"Meet me for breakfast tomorrow at the diner. We'll drive home from there. Do you know the diner?"

"I do. The Lake Effect Diner," Melanie said. "We'll be there. What time?"

"Eight o'clock."

The waitress appeared over Aaron's shoulder. "How are you folks doing?"

"Just fine," Jim nodded. "Just fine."

They parted company outside the bistro. The sky above the lake was dark, making the water indistinguishable from the land. Jim called Pat as he walked to his hotel.

"Hi, I'm walking to my hotel. It's a nice night."

"How was dinner?"

"Not bad."

"You are trying to hide a smile. I can hear it in your voice. Spill the beans."

"Spill the beans? I haven't heard that since, well, forever."

"Are you going to tell me or not?"

"I didn't eat alone."

"Melanie Johnson joined you for dinner."

"You're half right."

"The other half being...No kidding? Aaron Winters?"

Jim smiled for real. "Yep, Aaron is ready to turn himself in. We're driving to Cambridge tomorrow. Are you finally impressed with me, after all these years?"

"I am. Finally."

Jim paused at the entrance to his hotel and took one last look at the lake. He couldn't see the water but was close enough to hear it lapping against the shoreline. "Aaron's a lost soul who made a very foolish decision, but I can't help admiring him. To cut all ties to a father like Edgar is not easy."

"Mmm...by chance, does he remind you of anybody?"

"Yes, but my dad was ineffectual, not vindictive like Edgar. Even so, it took years for me to accept Dad as he was instead of resenting him for not being the father I wanted. I can't imagine how hard growing up must have been for Aaron, having an egomaniac for a father. Yes, and I acknowledge that my identifying with Aaron got in the way of solving this case, but please don't rub it in. All's well that ends well, as some minor writer said. Pat, I'm standing outside my hotel and the evening is getting chilly, so I'm going inside. I'll call again before I go to sleep."

"Goodnight, Jim. Well done."

He watched half of an early Law and Order, muttering expletives at the judge's rulings, and fell asleep with the TV on. He awoke in the middle of the night, realized what time it was, and texted Pat.

> Fell asleep watching Law and Order.
> Sorry I didn't call.

He dozed off but never really got back to sleep.

*

The three of them, Aaron, Melanie and Jim, had to wait ten minutes for a booth the next morning. Men in work boots and students with backpacks filled the diner. The smell of coffee and the sheen of vinyl – definition enough for a diner.

A booth felt great after the wait. "Who wants coffee?" a waitress asked. She carried a pot at the ready.

They all did. She poured steam and hot coffee into each mug. A fresh-faced young man dropped off menus without breaking stride. A waitress with a note pad asked, "Ready to order?"

"Give us a minute," Jim replied.

"We won't see her again for an hour," Aaron remarked after she left.

"Aaron, when we leave here I propose we drive straight to the DA's office and see Ted Conover, the Assistant DA.

He's a longtime friend of mine. He plays things by the book, but unlike some prosecutors he takes note of the human factor. He'll listen to you with an open mind. Next we will visit your father."

"Who will listen to me with a closed mind," Aaron said.

"Which is why I suggest we see Ted first."

"Should I come too?" Melanie asked Jim.

"You're welcome to drive down with us, but Aaron and I should visit the ADA and Aaron's father by ourselves. Ted will resent it if it looks like we're tugging on his heart strings. And Melanie's presence will set Aaron's father off. I predict he'll blame his son's behavior on you. 'No son of mine would do such fool things on his own,' he'll probably think, if not say."

Melanie looked plaintively at Aaron. "Are you okay with going alone?"

Aaron nodded. "The judge makes sense."

"So it's settled," Jim said. Aaron and I will drive to Cambridge when we leave here. I've already checked out of my hotel."

"Will I be locked up pending trial?" Aaron asked.

"I can't imagine that. My guess is that a date for arraignment will be set, but you'll be free on your own recognizance until then. It depends if Ted views your case primarily as a crime or primarily a domestic matter. That's my opinion, I could be wrong."

"You were a judge, you know the law."

"But I'm biased in your favor, and that may be affecting my judgement. Plus, your case presents a very unusual set of circumstances. There is nothing routine about it, no paint-by-numbers solution."

Melanie spoke with emotion. "Thank you for helping us, Judge Randall. I'm sorry I hid the truth from you."

"Melanie, I have to warn you, given your involvement, you will hear from Ted too. I don't think he'll throw the book at you, but you may be indicted."

The waitress appeared, glowering and tapping her order pad. "Are we ready to order?"

Jim glared back. "We have been ready for ten minutes."

The drive from Burlington to Cambridge was mostly on interstates. Aaron did little talking, and Jim was his usual gruff self – if he could change one thing about himself he would be more outgoing. As they crossed the Connecticut River into New Hampshire, Jim offered this advice to Aaron: when we're talking to Ted, don't be defensive or pugnacious. Ted has excellent radar and he'll see right through you; be straightforward and he will read you correctly. Got that?

"Yes, I do. How long have you two known each other?"

"Over twenty years. Ted argued a case in my courtroom when I was a brand new judge and he was a brand new Assistant DA. I was too unsure of myself to appreciate how unusual he was, but I came to realize that he has no hidden agenda. He just wants to do the best job he can. There's a tourist stop up ahead. I need to use the bathroom."

When Jim was finished using the restroom, he found Aaron in the gift shop looking at a New Hampshire map.

"Ready?" Jim asked.

Aaron pointed to the map. "I grew up in Cambridge, but I've never been to Lake Winnipesaukee. Can you imagine that?"

"Yes."

"Have you?"

"Been to Lake Winnipesaukee?" Jim asked.

"Yes."

"I went to camp there one summer. Didn't like it."

"Why not?"

"Too much outdoors. Shall we be on our way?"

Aaron replaced the map in the rack. "Let's go. I'm psyched."

Once they were back on the road, Aaron added, "I don't want Melanie to suffer for my decision. She tried to talk me out of it, but when she realized she couldn't, she agreed to help me." He made a sheepish face. "She loves me. Imagine that."

The closer they got to Cambridge, the more Jim questioned his motive in playing the middleman between Aaron and Ted. Yes, Jim's dad had been hard to reach, but Jim had never dreamed of feigning death to cut ties with him. Jim's way out was law school. He happened to like the law, or maybe he just lacked Aaron's guts.

"We'll go straight to Ted's office," Jim said, as he pulled off I-93 at the courthouse exit.

"Are you always this quiet?" Aaron asked. Jim hadn't spoken since they crossed the state line.

"Pretty much."

"Judge Randall, I regret dragging you into this. I truly do."

"Aaron, you got yourself into a hell of a mess and have no one to blame but yourself, but you've got the skills to make a real difference in life. You can pay me back by using your skills wisely when you've put this sorry episode behind you."

They had to park on the top floor of a parking garage. Jim had rarely driven to Ted's office since it was within walking distance of his townhouse. Having to find a parking space made the trip seem a bigger deal than when Jim walked.

Jim and Aaron had to wait in Ted's outer office.

"I'm scared shitless," Aaron whispered.

"Try to relax."

The door to Ted's office opened, and Ted ushered them in.

"Have a seat." Two chairs faced Ted's desk.

"Thanks for seeing us on such short notice," Jim said.

Ted sat behind his desk. "First thing I want to know, was Micky Owens's death a suicide?"

Aaron's voice faltered at first. He cleared his throat. "Micky knew that cancer was about to kill him. He wanted to leave his daughter money before he went, but he was ready to go. I assume he jumped from the bridge, but I don't know that for a fact."

"Okay, continue."

"But the kidnapping wasn't supposed to happen the way it did. Micky would confront me outside the coffee shop, that's how it was supposed to go. I wanted witnesses but had no desire to scare people. Micky's timing caught me by surprise. Dumb ass. Will I go to jail?"

"It's premature to talk about that. Tell me how you met Micky Owens."

"We met at the Middlesex Correctional Facility. I was volunteering to teach inmates computer coding."

Ted nodded. "I know the program. So you planned the abduction while Owens was in prison?"

"Yes. I had been scheming different ways to disappear before I met Micky, and the pieces fell into place after I got to know him and heard his story. When he learned he was to be released on compassionate grounds, we sealed the deal."

"The compassionate grounds being that he was dying."

"Yes. Micky decided to make the best of the time he had left by leaving money to Abigail, his daughter, whom he had neglected her whole life. All she needed to pay off the rest of her student loan was $3,000, so that's what he and I agreed on, and Melanie, my fiancée, loaned me the money. I don't want her to get in trouble."

"Again, premature to talk about. Continue."

Aaron glanced at Jim sitting impassively beside him. "We might have gotten away with it too, but Judge Randall wouldn't give up. I should hate him, but in a way I'm relieved. Melanie and I want to put this behind us and start our lives together."

Ted tapped his fingertips together. "You didn't think this through, did you?"

"Not entirely, no. Disappearing was the easy part, post-disappearance the hard part."

"Here's what is going to happen," Ted leaned forward. "You put a lot of law enforcement folks through a lot of unnecessary work. If you plead guilty and explain your circumstances, a judge may go easy on you. It's unlikely you'll do long time, although you may get to know the inside of prison from a different vantage point than when you taught coding to Micky Owens. I'm willing to let you walk out of here on your own recognizance, if you give me your word you won't try to flee before arraignment."

"You have my word."

"Have you spoken to your father?"

"We're on the way there now."

Ted said, "Good."

Jim muttered, "Punishment enough, I think."

Ted stood. Jim had never seen him look as stern. "No amount of potential, no amount of promise, can justify what you did, but it is clear to me that you are no threat to society. Work out your problems with your father, accept your punishment, then get on with your life. You owe that to all the people who searched for you when you disappeared."

"Yes, sir."

"I mean it."

"So do I. I am sincerely sorry for what I did."

"Jim, you'll make sure he shows up for the arraignment?"

"I will."

"Then we're done for now."

Jim and Aaron walked silently to the parking garage. Aaron had tears in his eyes.

"Are you okay?" Jim asked.

"I hate myself," Aaron said.

"Stop it! Stop it right now! You hear?"

"Why are you yelling at me?"

"Because you need to grow up. Don't give up your dreams, but think of others. You are not the only person on the planet."

They took the elevator to the roof of the parking garage, then drove down a corkscrew ramp to the street. MIT was not far away. Aaron called his father from the car.

"It's me, Dad. Yes, I'm alive and in Cambridge. Are you in your office? I'll explain when we get there. Judge Randall and I. Yes, he found me. Do you mind hearing me out before you yell at me? For once? Please?"

Aaron shook his head when he got off the phone. "Everybody's yelling at me."

"For good reason."

Jim found a parking space a block away from Edgar Winters's office, a small miracle. Aaron walked stiffly, girding for battle.

Edgar Winters didn't greet them warmly, let alone hug his son.

"Come in," he said.

"Dad, I can explain," Aaron said, advancing towards his father.

"This better be good." Edgar acknowledged Jim's presence, "Judge Randall."

"We just left the DA's office," Jim said. "Your son is not out of the woods, but he is being cooperative, and the DA will no doubt take that into account."

Edgar gestured to a small table in the corner of the room. "Sit."

Jim said, "I'm not staying. You two have a lot to talk about."

Aaron sounded plaintive. "You're not staying?"

"You need time with your father, lots of time."

Aaron looked panic-stricken.

"Aaron, this is your chance. Your dad will never fully understand what you did, but he needs to hear it directly from you – and as stubborn as he is, I think you have his attention."

Silence.

Edgar broke the silence. "The judge is half right, I'll never understand."

Jim replied, "But you need to hear Aaron out before you decide he's an unworthy son."

"I never thought he was unworthy. Misguided, bullheaded, but not unworthy."

"Good, that's a start. Now I'll leave you two alone. Aaron, I'll come with you to the arraignment if you want company."

"I'd like that, Judge Randall," Aaron said. "Thank you for all you've done."

"I think your father will be easier to manage now," Jim said.

Aaron and his father were still on their feet when Jim left the office. Edgar was leaning on the back of a chair. Aaron studied his father.

Jim retrieved his car and drove home. When he entered his house, he felt as if he had been away for years. He went into his kitchen and poured himself a glass of wine. The late afternoon sun seemed ready to call it a day.

He sat for a long time, sipping his wine, before he called Pat.

"It's me," he said when she answered.

"Are you home?"

"Yes, I just got here."

"How did it go?"

"As well as could be expected. I took Aaron to see Ted, then left him at his father's office. Aaron will be okay now. He won't find life or his father always accommodating, but he'll be able to cope."

"Are you in one piece?"

"I can't tell yet. It'll take me time to settle down. I'll never be the same, that's for sure. Staging your own kidnapping to escape the gravitational pull of your father no longer seems impossible. Which in itself is hard to grasp."

"Your voice sounds shaky."

"Being exposed to a man like Edgar Winters permanently warps one's view of human nature."

"I can't wait to see you, Jim."

"Can you come here? I'm exhausted."

"I'm on my way."

Made in the USA
Middletown, DE
25 February 2022